One Last Kiss

An Affair Without End

~Book 1 ~

Susan Ward

DEDICATION

For Three Special Authors I've met on my Journey:

Terri Lyndie, who is always kind, my go to girl for first read, and never fails to make me laugh in delight with her writing.

To Rachel Blaufeld, my ambassador of the blog who writes novels as steamy and sassy as she is.

And my little one, Fabiola Francisco, who writes such troubled girls and yet always puts a smile on my face.

Thank you so much for helping on this wacky road we've all taken. I would be lost and alone in technology without you and not laughing along the way as I do each day now with you girls!

CHAPTER ONE

1980

I storm out of the house and push my way through the swarm of drunken students. Somehow, I missed the rowdy cheer that followed the announcement that the cops have sealed off the roads, and the only way left out of this college town nightmare is the beach.

It's nearly impossible to navigate a path through the mob. A stream of beer hits my cheek and I hold up my hand to ward it off. The guy at the keg shoots the hose at me again and his buddies erupt into laughter. I reach the wooden steps over the cliffs and quickly descend to the beach.

Damn Rob. I should never have come to Santa Barbara with him. Spending Halloween hitting the college party scene was a definite mistake. It might be a good way to promote Rob's band, doing a gig at the biggest college town bash of the year, but it never stood a chance at being a good thing for me.

Why does Rob have to be such a jerk? We'd only been at the

party an hour before he decided the band should take a set break so he could sneak off with another girl. And the jerk doesn't even care that I caught him.

I sink into the sand and stare at the water. *What do I do now?* I could go back to the party and snag myself the first cute guy who looks at me and then rub it in Rob's face.

No, it's probably a better idea to take the car and ditch him here. Let him drive back to LA in that overcrowded, stinky van with the band. I should dump his clothes on the side of the road and get the hell out of Santa Barbara and back to the real world.

"Linda, what's wrong? Why did you run out of the party like you were being chased by demons?"

I look up to find Jeanette standing above me. So, she noticed my humiliating flight from the frat house.

I shrug. "Rob being Rob."

She shakes her head with an aggravated exhale that sounds like a growl.

She sinks down on the sand beside me. "God, Linda, what do you expect? You know how guys like Rob are? You need to get over this thing you have for musicians. It's not healthy. They all treat you like crap."

My eyes round and I fix on her a *back-off* kind of stare. "Thanks for the pep talk. We should do this again sometime real soon."

Jeanette shakes her head again. "I'm just saying you're better than the guys you date."

I spring to my feet and start to brush the sand from my legs. "I'm going for a walk. Don't follow."

I plod through the sand until I'm at the surf line.

"Linda, don't be this way. You can't take off at night alone on the beach. It's not safe. Let's just get the car and get out of here. Forget Rob. I'm not driving him back to LA after being such a jerk to you. You can do better."

I pretend not to hear her and continue to walk.

"Linda! Don't be this way."

I hurry down the coastline and Jeanette doesn't follow. She's knows better than to follow me when I am in *one of my moods* and I really don't want another chapter of her relationship advice. What does Jeanette know about being me?

She is beautiful; I am not. I'm sort of pretty, but I wouldn't say drop-dead-gorgeous like Jeanette. She is rich and I am not. She comes from a great family, and while Doris, my mom, is a pretty OK mom—no grievances there—I wouldn't call her "a great family."

My mom works as a waitress in Encino and still suffers from the delusion that my dad might return someday. He's been gone since before my birth.

I push my frizzy black hair from my face. Damn ocean air, the unavoidable frizz machine that can ruin even the best hair day. I'll look like Annie if I walk much longer, but I definitely don't want to go back to Jeanette and hear another of her lectures.

She thinks that my wayward trek through the LA musician population is just me trying to fill the hole left from being raised without a father. According to my roomie, I date loser musicians because my dad's music career was more important to him than me.

Nope, don't want to hear Jeanette's theories about my alleged abandonment issues.

I look over my shoulder and see that Jeanette must have

gone back to the party. Wrong again, roomie. I date only musicians because I'm trying to find my dad.

The sounds from the party become fainter with each step and I begin to slow my pace. The moon is high, brilliant and full, and the tide is low. It's one of those rare fogless nights and I'm grateful for it because I'm really not dressed for a dose of chilly ocean mist.

I wonder how long low tide lasts. If the tide starts to come in, I will never make it around the points along the coastline to get back to Isla Vista and Jeanette. I realize that I've walked so far that I've left the public beach and am now in an area of beachfront estates.

I look up at the massive homes on the cliffs, fully illuminated in the darkness. What must it be like to have enough money to let an entire house full of lights stay on through the night? Doris would get angry if I left lights on in the kitchen for five minutes.

I stop myself there, not wanting to dredge up the less pleasant parts of my childhood. I live in the dorms at USC thanks to my scholarship. I won't ever have to go back to that tiny condo in Reseda where I was raised.

The house ahead of me looks the length of an entire city block. I've never seen a house so big before. It's beautiful in Santa Barbara, like another world, happy and wealthy and safe. Yes, that's how it feels even walking alone at night on the beach. Small town, rich town safe. LA never feels this way, but then I never get beyond the parts where nothing ever looks like this.

I feel myself calm inside even though I haven't a clue what to do next. I don't even know where I'm walking to, but with the ocean on my right, it means I'm walking south, so at least I know I'm going in the right direction. LA is south.

I'll just sit for a spell, sort through what I want to do next about Rob, and then return to the party. I just don't want to go back. Not yet.

Up ahead of me, I spot two eucalyptus logs in the sand, resting close against the cliffs. The sand becomes deeper and more difficult to walk through away from the damp shoreline, but I stomp across it toward the weather-beaten logs.

I hear a sound. I freeze, scream, and jump back. The smaller log is moving.

Why is that log moving?

I see it isn't two logs; it's one log and one man lying in the sand. I try to get a better look at him in the darkness.

Is he OK? What is he doing here?

He moans. Maybe he fell on the stairs and banged his head. I hear what sounds like a bottle hitting wood. I exhale in heavy annoyance. He's drunk. The last thing I need to deal with tonight is another drunk male. Rob is enough drunk male for any one woman to have to deal with in a single lifetime.

I stare at him through the darkness. What am I supposed to do? I can't just leave him here. He looks pretty wasted, but only a stupid girl would try to help a drunk man on a beach, all alone, at night.

"Are you OK? Are you hurt?" I call out from a careful distance.

No response. I cautiously move towards him and peek over the eucalyptus log blocking him from clear view. All the muscles in my throat spasm at once.

Oh my!

This is no random, drunken bum. The man half-lit by moonlight is so perfect he looks unreal. He has golden waves of hair and, while it's longer than how most men his age wear it, I can tell it is neatly tended. His body is fit, long limbed, and tall. He looks like he must be over six feet.

It's then I notice he's lying just a few feet from the base of some poorly lit stairs that zigzag down from the cliffs. Does he live up there, in one of those magnificent houses overlooking the sea?

He's casually dressed—shoeless, a loose cotton shirt, designer jeans—but I can tell his clothes are expensive. A rich, gorgeous drunk out for a late night walk who passed out in the sand on his own private beach.

I take a step closer to him.

"Do you need help?" I ask.

Silence. I creep around the log until I'm closer. I must have blocked the moonlight before, because now I can see his face more clearly. My heart stops.

Oh my god, either my sanity has finally left me or that guy is a dead ringer for...

I shake my head to chase away my thoughts. It couldn't possibly be really him. There isn't a girl on earth who has ever been born lucky enough to find *him* alone on a beach. And I am anything but a lucky girl. It can't be him.

I sink down on the sand beside him. "Are you OK?"

"OK?" Dazzling blue eyes look up at me. "Of course, I'm OK. This is my beach. Why wouldn't I be OK?"

The perfection of his face makes the breath catch in my throat even as my face colors from the unexpected harshness in his voice. I shouldn't take offense. This man is more than a little drunk if the way he slurs his words is any indication.

I arch a brow and make a face. "Really. How lucky you are. I thought all the beaches in the California were owned by the state. Since you don't need help, I think I'll just sit here for a while and enjoy the crashing waves."

I hug my knees with my arms and I can feel him studying me.

"Who are you?" His eyes do a fast once over of the sheet tied around my body. "Or maybe I should ask what are you? A ghost? Why are you wearing a sheet?"

I have somehow forgotten I was dressed in a makeshift toga for the party. I fix my gaze on my sand-sprayed toes.

I shrug. "Perhaps I should ask why you are alone on the beach in the middle of the night drunk."

He eases up, balancing himself on his elbow, facing me. There is something innately sexy in the casual arrangement of his long body parts. The blood starts to pump even faster through my veins.

"Perhaps we can skip that part," he says in a hopeful way, more than a little charming.

I laugh. "Sure thing. It's nothing to me. I'm just a girl in a toga who wandered onto your beach. You don't owe me any answers."

He starts to laugh, brushing the golden blond hair from his face. "You're very funny, whoever you are."

I hold out my hand and smile. "I'm Linda."

He holds out his hand. "Jack."

The touch of his fingers sends a current rocketing through me. *Jack?* It's can't be. It has to be some kind of crazy coincidence.

I study his face more closely and begin to feel even shakier inside. Whoever this man is, he is gorgeous.

"So is this what you're going to do tonight? Just lie here alone on the beach?" I ask.

Those silky golden locks dance in the air as he shakes his head. "I'm not alone. I'm with you. A much better plan than I had twenty minutes ago."

There's just enough caress in his voice to give me butterflies. "And what was your plan before me?"

"I don't remember." He laughs and lies back against the sand.

I spring to my feet and give in to an impulse I'm certain isn't one of my wiser impulses. I hold out my hand to Jack.

"Why don't you let me take you home?" I point at the stairs built into the cliff. "Do you live up there?"

Jack's blue eyes begin to sparkle. "You want to take me home? Plan getting better each minute."

I roll my eyes. "I don't plan to stay there. I'm dropping you off and going on my way."

"In a sheet? Which way would that be? I might want to go your way instead of mine."

A smile teases at the corners of my lips. "I'm making sure you get home safely and then I'm going back to LA."

He grimaces. "Bummer. I hate LA."

He takes my outstretched hand and I have to roll my weight backward to help pull him to his feet. As he drops his arm heavily around my shoulders, we nearly crash to the ground. I realize his mind is working better than the rest of him.

I nod toward the stairs. "Up there?"

"Up there. Are you sure you can manage me? We could just sleep on the beach in your sheet."

I give him a stern look, but I can't completely contain my

smile. "You're not the first drunk I've ever had to deal with tonight, so keep your hands to yourself and don't be smart with me."

"No." He crosses his heart. "For the beautiful lady in the sheet, I'll be a perfect gentleman." He pauses at the base of the steps, moves a finger to my chin and turns my face so I can meet his eyes directly. "Unless you don't want me to be."

Oh lord.

This man is positively dangerous in how appealing he is in all moments, even this one, which definitely shouldn't make him endearing. And damn, if he doesn't know exactly his effect on women.

A touch of irritation mingles with the more pleasant sensations inside me. Whoever this man is, he is certainly a man-whore. He can run his game on a woman even drunk.

That puts him at the bottom of my list, even lower than finding him on the beach did.

I arch a brow and say in my best *not interested* voice: "I'll let you know when I get you the top of the stairs. My opinion of you might change after this, but I doubt it."

He laughs in a loose way. "I'm not going to ask if that means change for the better or worse."

"Smart move."

I help him up onto the first step, struggling to stay beside him. We do it again, up another step. The stairs are dimly lit, almost impossible to see, and yet somehow he can manage them well enough for the both of us not to go tumbling back to the beach.

By the time I reach the top, I'm breathing heavily, but Jack looks as if the climb hardly fazed him. My gorgeous drunk is definitely fit.

My eyes round as I stare at the single story Spanish mansion blazing with lights and the magnificently landscaped lawn. It's like Eden here. Jeez, what does this man do?

"This is your house?"

Jack laughs. "Yep. I'll introduce you to the neighbors on our second date."

"This is not a date."

"OK, we'll have it your way. I just wasn't sure what to call this encounter."

Encounter?

"This isn't a date. This isn't an encounter. Is there anyone home at your place?"

He gives me a teasingly hopeful look. "No. Why?"

I start guiding him forward toward the house. "Because if someone were home I'd just dump you on the lawn for them to find and take care of."

He laughs. "No you wouldn't. You're not that kind of girl."

"How would you know?"

He shakes his head. "If there is one thing I definitely know, it's women."

I decide not to probe that remark and to get away from Jack quickly. He is very alluring and I'm shocked to realize I'm attracted to him. But this is too weird of an adventure to pursue, even for me.

Though I must admit he is a remarkable find. One doesn't usually run across male prospects like this in the LA club scene. I can't recall the last time I ran across a man who was sexy, handsome, and obviously rich. I wonder what's wrong with him other than the drinking. There must be something, there always is.

I shake my head, frustrated with myself. Why am I critiquing him? He's just a drunk man I found on the beach. Besides, I'm not even certain he's serious, interested, or coming on to me. It might just be flirting. Handsome men flirt so much. It's in their DNA.

We half walk, half stumble, across the lawn. The feel of his weight on my shoulder is painful and the movements of his legs become less sure with each step.

I find the French doors into the kitchen unlocked and slide it open.

"Is there someone I should get for you?" I ask.

Jack shakes his head. "No one here. I told you that already."

I study his face. "Is that why you drink? You're alone in your big, fancy house?"

Jack gives a groggy laugh. "Not alone. Never alone."

His bloodshot gaze fixes on my face.

"God, you are beautiful," he whispers, touching my cheek.

My eyes widen.

Oh no.

I need to dump him in his bedroom and get out of here quickly. By the way he's looking at me, I can tell he's more than casually checking me out. Drunks are the most difficult kind of men to fend off and anything short of passed out drunk means I shouldn't assume he's unable to fuck.

"Let's just get you to bed," I say. We take a few more steps into what must be the living room. "Where is your bedroom?"

His shoulder hits me as he points down a hallway. His body sends me into a glass case and I grab onto it to keep from falling.

I freeze and stare. It's a guitar case and, even if I wasn't a fiend about the music history of the '60s, I would have recognized that famous CF Martin preserved in the glass case.

Lily, the guitar Jackson Parker took to Woodstock. My heart drops to my knees and then begins a frantic race. *It is him! Really him…*

I am breathless, unable to walk, unable to speak. Somehow after years of throwing myself at well-connected musicians, I've gotten into the belly of the beast.

I am in the *insider circle* within the recording industry, and I am alone with a man who might be able to help me find my father.

CHAPTER TWO

I continue guiding Jack down the hallway to his bedroom and fight to contain my inner excitement. It wouldn't be fair to pounce on him with what I want. I need to put him to bed, sober him up, and figure out how to stay here until morning so I can have a lucid conversation with him.

I lug him through the doorway and switch on the lights. For a moment I stop, breathless again. This is Jackson Parker's bedroom. I've been in a lot of musicians' bedrooms—too many bedrooms, Jeanette would say—but I've never been in a room like this before.

A massive king size bed sits facing a giant wall of glass with a stunning view of the ocean. Everything is spotless and subtly expensive, from the careless arrangement of rust and blue pillows on the bed, to the books and vinyl crowding the shelves, to the leather chairs positioned before the stone fireplace.

The artful arrangement of posh furnishings, memorabilia, and family photos has turned this large flowing space into something tastefully luxurious, homey and yet intimidating.

As we cross the bedroom, his hold on me grows tighter. He's practically an octopus and nearly impossible to work free from so I can put him onto the bed.

"Stop holding onto me. I need to put you down on the bed. You need sleep, Mr. Parker."

Jack frowns. "I need another drink and you can stop with that Mr. Parker stuff. Everyone just calls me Jack."

I guide him backward onto the bed and he takes me with him until I'm trapped across his chest. Jack laughs and the pleasant lines of muscles and warm flesh shimmy beneath me. His magnificent blue eyes lock on my face and begin to glow.

"I thought you'd never join me, baby," Jack whispers.

He touches my cheek with a finger. The scent of him surrounds me—even drunk the man smells good.

He tugs at my sheet. "All women should walk the earth wearing sheets. So sexy and convenient."

He reaches for the scarf around my waist that loosely holds my invention in place and I squirm in his grasp to stop his hand.

"Let's leave the sheet, shall we? I don't think you're going to be able to do much of anything in the shape you're in. Let me up. You need to sleep."

His expression softens into something sweetly regretful and almost tender. "I'm sorry that I'm drunk. I'm not usually like this. I promise."

I bite my lower lip and try to ease out of his arms. "Don't promise me. Promise yourself."

His hand falls away from me and his golden head wobbles on the pillow.

Now what? I don't know what I should do. Do I put a blanket over him? Do I run from the room? Or do I just sit in a chair and watch this iconic genius sleep?

I sink down on the edge of the bed and just stare. How dazzling he is. The most beautiful man I've ever seen. I feel my flesh tingle.

I pull a blanket from the foot of the bed up and over him.

"You're not leaving, are you?" he whispers.

I shake my head.

"No. We'll talk in the morning, but now sleep."

"Linda, Linda, Linda. Where did you come from? Why are you here?"

"Aha. So you remember my name."

"Of course, I do." He frowns.

"I came from that way." For some lame reason I point. "North."

Jack chuckles. "That's not north. That's west. The beach faces south here."

"Then it's a good thing I found you. If I continued to walk the shoreline I might have ended up in New York. I was going east without knowing it. I would have never reached Los Angeles that way."

He laughs. "Beautiful and funny. Why LA?"

"It's where I live."

His golden brows pucker into a frown. "So why are you in Santa Barbara wandering the beach all alone wearing a sheet?"

"I'm not alone. I went to a party with my roommate. It's not far from here."

I reach under the lampshade to turn out the light.

"Roommate? Male or female?" he asks.

"Female, not that it's any of your business."

"Then she won't miss you tonight."

And before I know what he's doing, I am in his arms being turned beneath him on the bed. His face descends before I can stop him and Jackson Parker is kissing me.

The touch of his mouth shoots through my body like an electric current and it feels like I'm completely surrounded by the warm length of him. With gentle demand, his lips ease apart my lips and I feel the lightest touch of his scotch-flavored tongue against my mouth. One hand slips beneath my sheet to caress my breast.

His hand begins to glide over my flesh as if he's relishing and absorbing the feel of me. His movements are erotic and sure, almost leisurely. Their effect on me is anything but leisurely. Every speck of my skin is heating rapidly and he is only kissing my lips while his hands calmly roam my flesh.

My breath catches in my throat. Who would have expected a man like Jackson Parker to take with such heart-melting gentleness?

I try to work free of him. The man definitely knows how to get a woman from zero to sixty in record time. As much as I want to stay until he sobers—and my alert senses taunt me that *this* would be a surefire way to ensure *that*—it wouldn't be a good thing for either of us. I'm not even sure he's aware of whose body is beneath him.

"Jack..." I moan into his lips.

His face lifts and his blue eyes begin to glow. "Say my name again, lovely Linda—" his voice is a sensual rasp, "—and then no more words. Just me being good to you. You being good to me. Two strangers from the beach in an encounter we both want."

His mouth lowers back to me and I feel like I am melting into the bed. As his mouth plunders mine, what's in his kiss is something I've never felt before, a hungry desperation with whispers of longing. He kisses me as if we've shared a thousand kisses, as if he knows the contour of my lips and what pleases me: the touch of his tongue against mine, the gentle swirls that dance and play, and even the light nips of his teeth on my lower lip. His moves, knowing and sure, are beguiling and pulling me into him.

He rolls back from me until he is kneeling, and then the tie on my sheet is gone. *Jesus Christ, how did he get my toga off me without me stopping him?* I'm lying totally naked, except for my panties, and Jackson Parker is making love to me with his famous blue eyes.

His gaze roams me in the same unhurried fashion as his hands. He smiles at me, his expression soft. "Fuck, you are beautiful, Linda. I knew those big brown eyes would never lead me false."

He pulls off his shirt without unbuttoning it and tosses it on the floor.

The muscles in the deepest part of me clench and my velvet flesh feels like it is dripping—just from sight of his chest in this erotic fantasy.

I stare at him in spellbound wonder. It's not possible for another man to be so confident and sexy and hypnotic.

In a single, fluid glide he removes my panties. I look away, trying to control the flash-fire in my body.

He laughs, starting to work on the fastenings of his jeans. "Don't stop looking, Linda. Look. Touch. Do what you want. It's all good with me."

Do what I want?

I bite my lower lip and I can feel that my eyes are enormous as I stare up at him. I want to fuck this man hard, right now, until I've pounded every other musician I've ever been with out of my head, until Jackson Parker is the only memory I have of sex. We haven't even started, but I can feel it, that this is going to be mind-blowingly indescribable.

Leaning down, he kisses me until I am breathless and pliant in want of him. He starts to ease off his jeans, somehow still kissing across my jaw, my chin, my neck. I hear the sound of denim hitting the floor, and I want to look at him, but his kisses have moved to the swell of my breasts. His golden head blocks my view of the rest of him.

And then he's up on his knees, gazing at me, and I flush because he is everything a man should be and too often isn't. Every inch of him is fit, tanned, virile, ready and larger than life.

What the hell was he doing alone on the beach at night for me to find? My blood is pumping through my body, and being here with him is so unexpected and so hot in its surrealness.

He scoops me up in his arms and lifts me from the bed into him, his erection pushing into me as his mouth reclaims mine demandingly. Gripping his upper arms, I surrender to this fast-moving shift into scorching passion. His body is strong and muscular, his hands flex on my backside, and I eagerly stroke against his hardness with my moist, soft flesh. I want him so badly, and tentatively I move my hands to feel his face, his hair, the pulse beating in his neck.

I kiss him there, and he arches me backward, touching the tip of his erection against my vagina, and then he moans, setting me down upon the bed. His fingers hold my hips as he runs his tongue around my navel. Then, with gentle nips and swirls of his tongue he traces a path between my hipbones. His breath is brushing my mound. His eyes are fixed on my perfectly shaved lower parts and his finger lightly glides my labia.

My hand strays to his hair, my fingers lacing into his golden waves, and his face turns, his blue eyes glittering with desire.

"I love the way you smell," he whispers, and I nearly convulse at the look of pure pleasure in his eyes. He kisses me on my mound. "I bet you taste just as wonderful."

Before I can react, he is there, mouth, fingers, everything. I gasp as he runs his tongue along the inside of my fold, away from me, across my vagina and then blows. One hand moves to my breasts, his callused fingers stroking my hardened nipple. His mouth sweeps up the other side of me and then pauses to lightly flick and tease my clitoris.

I groan, arching on the bed, and he chuckles. Even his laugh is erotic, stirring the air across my sensitive nerve endings.

"Oh, Linda, you need this even more than I."

His tongue flutters against me clitoris. My thighs begin to shake.

"Do you like that?"

I nod. His mouth works greedily this time, consuming my juices and making me ooze even more. His tongue runs up my mound, swirls and lifts.

"Or do you like that better?"

There is no point answering him, he already knows the answer, but I nod anyway. His mouth lowers and my fingers tighten around the sheets.

My head rolls back on the pillow and my hips begin to move in urgency against him. I feel heat and sensation along my nerves, building impatience, as his mouth devours my need. I want to savor this, prolong it. He's only just started and I'm almost about to come. I can't even remember the last time a man gave me an orgasm and he's doing it with expert sureness.

I arch, my body twitching, my fingers tightening in his hair, and I feel a blow and then his tongue leaves me.

"Oh please, don't stop," I beg. I open my eyes to find him hovering over me as I squirm with need.

"Never," he murmurs before leaning down to kiss the inside of my thigh. Another shockwave through my muscles. My skin is burning and I need his mouth there, but he is kissing the flesh of my thighs, my pelvis, near and then away, but never there. I feel like I'm about to crawl out of my skin.

He slips a finger slowly into me. He begins to work with his mouth as his finger is lifted for me to taste me. He swirls it in my mouth, the taste of me and the taste of his flesh. I'm clenching tighter and tighter, my breasts swell, my nipples harden even more, and every single nerve ending in my body explodes at once.

His mouth closes completely over me as I convulse against his tongue. His is kissing me, sucking me, licking me as my cries shatter the silence of the room.

It keeps going on and on. I can't breathe and there is too much sensation. It is too intense all at once. I try to move my hips away, but he holds me there, getting more aggressive in delivering me pleasure.

It feels like someone has covered me with oil and lit me on fire. The quaking should have started to calm, but it is intensifying. My arousal shifts, building like I'm going to come apart again.

I'm lost in my own breathing and roiling flesh. My breath is still ragged as I rally enough to open my eyes. Jack is on his hip, reclined beside me, staring down at me with a smile of pure satisfaction.

"Your body is wonderfully responsive." He scoops me from the bed, turning me into him. He starts kissing me on the neck. "But you don't know a thing about letting yourself enjoy pleasure, do you?"

There is no time to react. I am draped across his body and he is slowly lowering me onto his erection. My flesh swallows him deeply and I instantly shudder and tighten around him. Briefly, he closes his eyes and his breathing hitches.

He doesn't move. He eases up into me, taking a breast in his mouth, and I want to ride him hard. I try to move. He stills me. His tongue swirls around my nipple as he slowly moves his cock out and then back in, somehow even deeper. His mouth sucks harder. I roll my hips. He stops me.

"Don't move your body," he whispers, holding my hips steady as he lies back against the pillow. "Just let me move you."

He slides me up the length of him slowly, knowing exactly how to glide inside me so all the most sensitive parts are stroked. He lowers me in delicious increments. My body quivers as my back arches and my thighs clutch.

I start to shake. I try to grind and ride his cock. He lifts one hand to touch my cheek. With the other he stills my anxious limbs.

"Oh no, lovely Linda. Tonight I want to please you."

Oh my.

He moves inside me, whispering my name, holding me captive to his body and his touch and his kisses. All parts of me are completely absorbed into him and I am lost in the feel of a man for the first time in my life.

CHAPTER THREE

I wake smelling of Jack and sex, wondering how I got here.

I haven't been a virgin since I was fourteen, but those hours in Jack's arms felt like a second virginity loss. At last, I have experienced what sex should be.

Cheeks burning, I turn on my pillow to find him sleeping beside me. He is even more gorgeous washed in morning light with his lax features and tousled, bright hair. My gaze greedily roams the parts of him not hidden beneath the sheets.

He is magnificent. A man at his peak and prime of masculine appeal. Not young. Not old. Just the perfect blend of both that no woman could resist.

I note the time on the clock resting on the bedside table and resist the urge to kiss him. Ten a.m. I better call Jeanette at the motel before she sends the police out looking for me. *Jeez, she's going to be pissed.* Not only did I ditch her last night, I left her alone to deal with Rob.

I shake my head, mind made up and determined. Rob: over, finished, gone. A giant waste of my time in more ways than one.

Even if I didn't have very fresh memories of how a man *should* treat a woman in bed—thanks to Jack—I would have ended us anyway after that stunt he pulled at the party.

I don't take shit from any man.

Careful not to wake Jack, I ease to the side of the bed and sit up. I reach for his shirt and my panties lying on the floor and my eyes lock on a collection of photos sitting on a table.

I pull on my clothes and make a detour on my trip to the bathroom, stopping at the table. Family photos. I lift what must surely be a 24-carat gold picture frame and stare at the woman preserved in glass.

Lena Parker. Jackson Parker's dead wife. I don't need anyone to explain to me who she is. Even if I wasn't a knowledgeable groupie, Lena had been enormously famous in her own right.

If ever a woman had it all, it was Lena Parker. Beautiful, talented, a world-renowned violinist, perfect husband—I look around the room—perfect home, wonderful children. What a tragedy that she died so young.

It's been four years. Is that why Jack drinks? The loss of her? I set the picture down and lift up another one, and everything inside me goes cold.

Oh Christ.

I stare into the time-frozen image of Sam Parker, Jackson's son. I remember Sammy well. I used to see him play with his band in the LA club circuit. A brilliant guitarist and an amazing voice. He was definitely a star on the rise. Sexy as all hell, but troubled and dark. He just died last spring from a drug overdose and they found him in his bedroom here in this *oh-so-perfect* house.

A snippet from the tabloids stirs in my memory. Jack has existed in total seclusion since he buried his son. I wonder why he should let me someone like me, a strange girl from the beach, into his carefully guarded world.

Perhaps the pressures of being alone in his sorrow has grown too much for him. Perhaps it is only intimacy with a stranger he can manage, and that's why I'm here. I am nothing to him and maybe that's my appeal. It wouldn't be the first time a man used me this way.

I set the picture back onto its resting place. I focus on the little girl. She has to be Jack's daughter. Same golden hair. Same dazzling blue eyes. How sweet she looks, but sad.

Most musicians have a sad tale, but Jack's history is sadder than most. I suddenly feel badly about being here and why I want to stay.

I slip into the bathroom and quietly close the door.

Oh fuck, is this how rich people bathe?

I stare at the room in wonder. It's larger than my mother's living room, with an enormous sunken tub before a wall of glass, a separate dual-stream shower, and double sink vanity. There is even room for a chaise, a full wall mirror for dressing, and a special lighted vanity dressing table.

OK, where's the toilet?

I open a door. A linen closet. I open another and there it is. I lift the lid, pull down my panties and sit to pee. The phone mounted on the wall makes me laugh.

You're not in Reseda any more, Linda.

I unroll paper from the fancy, custom design TP holder.

I flush, put down the seat, sit and reach for the receiver. I dial 411 for the number to our Santa Barbara motel.

When it's answered I ask the front desk for my room, and then listen to it ring.

"Hello?" says a clearly irritated Jeanette.

I scrunch up my face. "Hi, roomie. Everything OK?"

Silence. Not one of the swifter things I could have said, but I can already tell that Jeanette is seething.

"Linda. Where the hell are you? I've been worried sick. You didn't come back to the party and I searched the beach for you for hours. How can you just ask me if everything is OK? Are you thoughtless or out-of-your mind?"

"I don't know. You tell me. You're the psychology major." Second lame remark, but the best defense is always a good offense, so I ask, "How's Rob. Is he pissed at me?"

I hear a heavy, aggravated exhale through the receiver. "Thank you for asking about me. And I'm pissed at you, in case you were wondering. And Rob. I don't know how he is. I left him at the party with that girl he was making the moves on."

"That's probably for the best," I say.

Silence.

Then Jeanette says, "I'm packing up and driving back to LA within the hour. Do you want me to pick you up? Do you plan to stay? Not that I care, but what are you doing and who are you with? I should probably know that in case we find your body on a beach later."

OK, I deserved that. This isn't the first time I've ditched Jeanette and gone off with a guy.

"Well, if you must know, I hit on Jackson Parker on the beach last night and I fucked him until dawn."

Jeanette's laughter is harsh, disbelieving and insulting.

"There is no need to get nasty and vulgar," she says, in that superior way she has at times. "You know I hate the gutter mouth. The guys you hang out with might think it's sexy, but I think its crude. Really, where are you? Should I pick you up?"

I make an angry grimace. I decide to lie, tell her something she'll believe just to get rid of her. "I'm still in Isla Vista. I'm going to hang around for a while. I'll be home next week."

"What about your things? Do you want me to drop them off?"

"Don't bother. I wouldn't want to inconvenience you," I say and hang up.

The second I set down the receiver, I realize my mistake. I shouldn't have said that and slammed down the phone on her. Now I won't have my purse or my clothes.

Crap, but that's Jeanette. No one can piss me off and knock me off my feet faster. I've just hit the mother lode and my roomie can be such a downer.

I've never met a girl in the LA scene who can brag she's had Jackson Parker. It's like entering the groupie hall of fame, not that my roomie would appreciate that.

I stop at the sink to wash my hands and face. My teeth feel positively gross and I debate whether to use Jack's toothbrush. It's kind of a disgusting thing to do, but I use it anyway. It's better than having beer-and tequila shooter-tainted morning breath.

I gargle and rinse. I run my tongue along my teeth. I cup my hand in front of my mouth and breathe out. Better. Much better.

I find a brush on the counter and try to do something with my hair, but it's pointless. It's still transformed into tightly curled ringlets with pockets of frizz. With a tissue I dab away the smudges of mascara beneath my eyes.

I study myself in the mirror, then feel ready to go back in the bedroom and move this encounter the direction I need to take it.

My steps become more purposeful as I near the door. It's absolutely necessary that I take full charge of this opportunity. I don't want Jackson Parker brushing me off before I can learn if he can help me find my father.

I open the door, step out, and freeze.

Oh Jeez. He's awake, reclined against pillows, and staring right at me. How is it possible for a man to look so good after a night of drinking and sex?

He takes a long drag of his cigarette, slowly exhales and studies me through the smoke. The Marlboro man has nothing on him.

"So you *are* real…and very beautiful," he whispers approvingly. "I wasn't sure I didn't dream you."

The blood instantly begins to heat in my veins. I make a face. "Nope, I'm real."

He stares at me and then smiles. "Oh, better than real. A man can get lost looking into eyes like yours."

I feel my insides shudder and I struggle to catch my breath.

I hang back, watching him smoke, and try to plan my next move. He hasn't called me by name. Does even know who I am? Is that his game with the sexy talk? He's bluffing his way through the morning after of a night he doesn't recall?

"How much of last night do you remember?" I ask.

Jack takes a long drag of his cigarette. "All of it." His eyes rove me leisurely. "Some of it." Another drag. A laugh. "The good parts. What answer would you prefer, Linda?"

I laugh. He's fast on his feet in the morning. I'll give him that.

"Do you remember us meeting?" I ask.

He frowns. "Of course. I don't get picked up by many women wearing only a sheet. What was that about anyway? Who wears a sheet to a party?"

My eyebrows shoot up. Pretty fast recollection of events. "It was a toga party," I explain, indignantly. "Do you remember me brining you home?"

His eyes start to glow. "Do you want me to remember or do you want me to forget?"

I decide a bold play of my own. "Depends. Are we still having an encounter or is this now a date?"

The smile that flashes on Jack's face is heart-stoppingly sexy. He puts out his cigarette.

"Which answer gets you back into bed?"

Oh, there we go. Right question. Right direction.

I feel my pulse tick up in beat. "Encounter. Oh, definitely encounter."

He turns down the sheet, invitingly. "A woman after my own heart. Come here."

I make another fast decision on how to keep control of this. I don't climb into bed. I sit on my knees, atop the covers, beside him.

Jack's smile is amused. "So, how long are you staying?"

My eyes round in surprise.

"What? Do you just pick up women randomly and expect them to stay."

"Nope, you'd be the first in a very long time so I'm a little rusty at this. I just like to roll with my encounters. See where they go."

The laughter pushes upward inside of me—*God, this man*

oozes charm with every breath—but I can't let him know he can charm me or he'll have total control in this.

I crinkle my nose. "Is that some sort of '60s free love kind of philosophy?"

He cups my chin with a hand and lightly moves a finger along my jaw. "Don't knock it until you've tried it, Linda. Some of the best things in my life have come from random moments I've least expected."

"Then, you're lucky. Most of my random moments end up scaring the hell out of me."

He brushes my lower lip with his thumb and everything below my waist comes alive. "Maybe your luck is changing, Linda. I'm your last random moment, and I think it's going pretty well so far."

He's leaning into me, and I don't know whether to run with the moment or change course.

My resistance melts away at the first touch of his lips. As wonderful as the searing passion had been last night, it cannot compare to this clear-headed, enticing seduction.

No man has ever kissed me this way. A disarming blend of lust and tenderness. Part man, part boy. And of all men to kiss me this way, it has to be Jackson Parker: part sex symbol, part aging superstar, part dream, and part misery.

I am beneath him on the bed before I realize he brought me there. I feel his warm flesh all around me. His boldness and gentleness urge me onward, giving me the courage to get lost in him and take what I want.

My tongue slips through his parted lips, and he answers with a blissful, swirling dance. He doesn't make love in parts, it is all of him always at once, not fast and not slow, a perfect rhythm of flesh and desire and him.

The taste of his flesh is as beautiful as he is, and my mouth wanders the perfect lines of his face, sipping and memorizing the line and texture. A throaty laugh shudders from deep inside his throat as our mouths continue more hungrily—and it is then I realize I am kissing him, I am consuming him and he wants it this way.

Heated currents surge through my body. He moves our bodies with artful sureness into a perfect fit, my curves against his muscles, his warm flesh against my smooth skin, my yielding sex to his hardening sex.

He lowers his mouth, kissing from my lips to a taut, rosy peaked breast. As he caresses it with his tongue, I moan, threading my fingers through his hair. As quickly as we are moving it feels almost like slow motion. As primal as the urge is, it is sweetly giving.

I arch up, no longer able to endure the play on my breasts without his flesh within me.

Jack laughs and lifts his head, mesmerizing blue eyes locking on mine. "You are too impatient. You need to learn patience, how to savor your own senses."

He takes one of my nipples into his mouth, brushing it feather-lightly with his tongue, with the slightest suck. He moves away from me. That part of me dripping and eager begins to pulse fiercely.

He moves downward to my navel. Against my flesh, he whispers, "Slowly, lovely Linda. We have all day."

I relax into his touch and uncharacteristically obey. If there is heaven on earth, it is Jackson Parker making love to me his way.

CHAPTER FOUR

I lift my chin from Jack's damp chest. He is definitely a morning sex kind of man and even better in the light.

He smiles at me. I sense he is more than a little lonely and in need of this.

With a long, tanned index finger, he pushes back a wayward hair from my cheek. "You have sage eyes."

Jeez, I don't know how to take that one. He's a difficult man to read.

I make a face. "My eyes are brown, not green. I'm not sure if I should take that as a compliment."

Jack laughs. "I meant it as a compliment. Your eyes are wise." He kisses me gently on the lips. "You've seen a lot for a girl so young, you carry it in your eyes, and yet you are one of the gentlest women I've ever run across. And definitely kind."

I blush and lay my cheek back against his chest. "How do you know? You just met me. Maybe I'm not kind at all. Maybe I'm just looking for a story to tell my girlfriends. Maybe I just want get laid by a musical genius with a really hot body for his age."

Jack laughs harder. "Thanks a lot. I'd be completely offended if not for the hot body part." His laughter ebbs, and with a graceful quickness of hand he lifts my face. "Don't be flippant. I'm being serious here. You're a pretty amazing woman."

I trace my finger along his chest, sidestep the compliment because compliments make me uncomfortable, and debate with myself whether to ask.

I kiss his chest and then look up. "Why were you drunk last night? I read somewhere you've been sober for ten years."

Jack exhales heavily and runs a hand through his hair. "An alcoholic is an alcoholic forever. We don't need reasons to drink. It was a relapse. Reasons are crutches to enable drinking. I prefer to focus on the reasons not to drink."

I study his expression. "You seemed very sad at times. Why were you sad?"

Jack frowns. "Do you really want to know?"

I nod.

His arms tighten around me, tucking more closely against him. "It's hard being alone in this house with my regrets. It caught up with me last night. It was my son's birthday."

My eyes grow large.

Jack sighs. "We all make mistakes, Linda. We all have to live with them."

I rub my cheek against the flesh above his heart. "I'm sorry. I shouldn't pry. Everyone says I'm curious to the point that I'm rude."

He lifts my chin. "Not rude. You're a caring person. That's a rare thing to find these days."

"How can you say that? You don't even know me."

"I don't know you, huh?" He pulls out of my arms until he's sitting cross-legged on the bed. He studies my face. "You are twenty-one years old tops, though you try to act older, and you try to act tough so people won't see how unsure and easily hurt you are. You're in college somewhere. Either working your way through school or on scholarship. You're very intelligent. I'm betting on scholarship. Someone hurt you really badly. You carry that pain. It's in your eyes. And because of that you let men use you, you give yourself cheaply, when all you really want is to somehow end the pain."

My entire face is burning by the time he's done. How the hell can he see that? Nearly perfect in every observation. Inside my head, I see Jeanette nodding in agreement.

He smiles. "I've told you. There is one thing I know. Women. But more than that, it's troubled souls. I read those pretty well too."

A touch irritated and enormously defensive, I snap, "How boring people must be for you, being able to see everything and never needing to know anyone. You can live the rest of your life completely alone with only random encounters because you read us all so well and we must bore you."

Oh crap, I just zapped back with a knee-jerk reaction. I can tell by the look in his eyes I definitely hit him with that. *Damn. Why did I do that?* The last thing I need is to give him a reason to make me go.

There is a heavy silence in the room that's nearly crushing. Then Jack smiles and reclines on a hip.

"So, where do you go to school?" he asks casually.

My eyes round, as I was not expecting that calm inquiry.

"USC. And if we'd bet money, you would have won. Full scholarship."

"What do you study?"

"Why are you asking? Do you really want to know this?"

"Sure I do. You're an interesting woman. I can only read you—" Jack holds up his thumb and index finger with just a hair's space between them. "—this much."

"I'm an English major. But I don't know why. I had to pick something because of my scholarship."

"See, that one surprised me. I would have thought a girl like you would have a carefully thought out plan. Isn't there something you wanted to study?"

"I used to dance."

"Exotic?"

I hit him in the bicep, even though I can see he's teasing. He curls away from me for a second, laughing.

"No. Ballet. But I blew out a tendon." I point to my ankle. "Pretty much ended my dancing career." I lift my chin. "I wanted to be a ballet dancer."

Jack kisses me lightly on the lips. He eases back, smiling. "You certainly have a dancer's body."

I crinkle my nose. "Is that a polite way of saying I'm flat chested?"

He gives me a mockingly chastising look and climbs from the bed. "Your body is perfect. What isn't perfect is how you see yourself."

I watch him pull on his jeans.

"Where are you going?"

"To make you breakfast." He checks the clock. "Or maybe I should say lunch. You are hungry, aren't you? I'm starved."

I nod. He drops a kiss on my mouth.

"Why don't you take a bath and clean up while I cook for you?"

He crosses the room and disappears into a closet. He returns carrying some clothes and lays them on the bed.

"These should fit you. Pick what you like. If you're going to stay here for a while, I'll need to take you shopping. But we can't go shopping with you wearing a sheet, not even in Santa Barbara."

I follow him with my eyes as he moves to the door.

"You're an interesting man, Jackson Parker. I don't know what to make of you."

Those stunning blue eyes lock on me. "Don't make anything, Linda. Let's just have a little fun."

Bathed and dressed, I make my way down the long hallway, finally finding the kitchen. The house is confusing as hell. Room after room, and none of it laid out logically. A lot of wasted space, in my opinion. Rich people can afford to waste space.

I take in the kitchen with a quick glance since I really didn't notice much about it last night. Marble counters, custom backsplashes, expensive dark wood cabinets and high-end appliances. Above the sink, another giant wall of glass reveals an ocean view.

Everything perfect, nothing vulgar or ostentatious, *just like him*. The blood instantly begins to heat in my veins when I spot Jack at the breakfast bar. I watch him carefully butter toast, slice it in two, and set in on the plates.

He really is making me breakfast.

I clear my throat. Nervous, I hold my arms wide. Jack whirls from counter.

"I think I should be making breakfast," I announce. "I look like June Cleaver in this."

Laughing, Jack sets down the knife and smiles. "You look lovely, Linda."

I stare down at the pink flowered, out-of-style, mid-calf dress. "Didn't your wife own any jeans? I'm assuming that these are her clothes and not some sort of costume for naughty role playing or something."

He looks amused. "No role playing. My wife's. And no jeans. Not that I know of. Lena was a very elegant woman. I don't think I ever saw her in jeans. You're welcome to look if you'd like."

I crinkle my noise. "To be honest, I would rather not be wearing this."

He drops a kiss on my nose. "To be honest, I'd rather you not be wearing it as well." The roguish glint in his eyes makes it perfectly clear how I should take that one.

A smile forces its way through my indignant composure. "That's not what I meant."

"I know. But I can't take you out shopping in a sheet. You have to wear something."

He studies my outfit and something flitters across his face— is that pain? What man keeps his dead wife's possessions for nearly four years? What kind of man is Jackson Parker?

I touch his cheek. "I'm sorry. This must be as strange for you as it is for me."

"Just a little." He steps back, as if something all the sudden makes him need space between us. He settles against the counter.

Abruptly, he asks, "How do you feel about wearing something of the housekeeper's? You look about the same size as Maria."

From dead wife's to maid's clothes. *Great, Linda, you're hitting a home run here.* Less creepy but still icky.

I smile and sink into my chair at the table. "Beggars can't be choosers. I'm the one who ran off wearing only a sheet."

"Wait here."

I cut into my eggs as Jack hurries from the room. I take a bite. They're really good, spicy from sautéed peppers and some kind of red sauce. I take another bite and then reach for my toast.

Jack returns. "Success. Jeans and a few other things you might prefer. I put them on the bed for you."

I watch him sink into the chair across from me and he fills his coffee cup.

We eat in silence for several minutes, and the silence feels strange after the closeness of the morning in bed together. I wonder if something is bothering him...or maybe it's having me here.

I watch him take a bite of his eggs.

"Do you want me to go?"

Jack looks up, startled. "No. Why would you ask that?"

"I don't know. It just feels like something has changed. I don't want to overstay my welcome."

Shaking his head, he reaches for his coffee. "Stay, Linda. Stay as long as you like. I mean that. I don't do things I don't want to do."

"OK." I set down my fork and lean back in my chair. "But why are you being so nice to me? Helping me out of this stupid jam I've put myself in. Making me breakfast. Taking me shopping. I'm nothing to you."

Jack looks amused. "Why are you so suspicious? Why can't we just be what we are? And why can't we just roll with it?"

"Because I've never met anyone who is kind without a reason."

"You are," Jack counters swiftly. "Besides, I consider us friends. That makes you important to me."

Friends? Jesus Christ, I just met the man last night and not exactly in a normal way. How can he say any of that with straight-faced sincerity? He is either the weirdest musician I've ever met or absolutely the best smooth-talker.

He collects his plate. "Are you finished?"

I nod and hand him my plate. He goes to the sink and starts washing everything he just dirtied to make us breakfast. I watch him, trying to figure him out.

He looks over his shoulder and those potent eyes lock on me. "There are no chance meetings, Linda. Every person who comes into your life comes into your life for a reason. You just have to be receptive to finding the reason."

I move from the table to the sink, grab a towel, and hold out my hand for the pan he just finished rinsing.

"Where did you learn that? A commune?"

Jack laughs. "You do have a sassy mouth on you." His gaze begins to sparkle. "Are you trying to insult me or trying to charm me?"

I blush. I bite my lip. "I'm not sure."

He puts a light kiss on my lips. "Go change. Let me finish this and take a shower so we can get out of here for the day."

CHAPTER FIVE

I stand in the open garage watching as Jack carefully puts down the top on the black 450 SL Mercedes.

"We're going to drive around town with the top down?" I ask.

Jack smiles. "Of course. It's a beautiful day. Why shouldn't we?"

"Don't people bother you when you go out?"

"These are my neighbors. Why would they bother me?"

"Because you're a fucking living legend," I say, not able to refrain from pointing out the obvious.

Jack laughs. "Oh." And as overtly amused as he is by me, he leaves that one alone.

I go to my side of the car and attempt to help by pretending to know what I'm doing, but I've never been so close to a car that cost this much, let alone touched one.

He comes around and gently moves me out of the way. He starts to fix the mess I made trying to secure the top down on the passenger side.

"Why do you swear so much?"

I shrug. "Shitty upbringing, I guess."

Jack stares at the heavens as if begging for patience. I bite back a smile.

He opens my door. "Whoever raised you did a wonderful job. Except for the tough-girl chip on your shoulder and the swearing."

I drop into my seat. "There is that."

He leans in to lightly kiss me on my lips. "There is a lot more than that to you, Linda."

My insides shudder and I can feel my eyes sparkling. As I pull the lap belt over the jeans I've appropriated from the housekeeper, I watch Jack go around the car and sink into his seat beside me.

He reaches into the backseat and pulls out two baseball caps. He hands one to me.

"What's this for?" I ask as I take the hat. I arch a brow in mock suspicion. "Trying to hide me from view?"

He shakes his head as reaches into the glove box for two sets of sunglasses. "Put the hat and glasses on. You'll thank me later when your face isn't burned and you haven't spent hours fighting your hair."

I nod and obey, dropping down the visor mirror so I can fix my hair into something not too awful with the hat.

He puts the car into gear and backs out of the garage.

"Where are we going?" I ask.

"Don't know yet."

At the end of the driveway, I get my first glimpse of the neighborhood and my eyes widen. Everything is beautiful, woodsy and natural. The narrow road cuts between modest estates tucked behind high stucco walls or split rail fences.

There are more trees lining the rolling hills and road than I would see in a year in LA, providing a sheltering umbrella as we whiz down the curving lane. Gates, dogs, horses, and money.

Out of the corner of my eye, I watch Jack as I pretend to study the scenery. Why is he taking me shopping and acting like he wants me to stay? Usually, the bigger the star the faster they can't wait to show me the door in the morning.

The sex is great between us, but I still can't figure out why someone like Jackson Parker is letting me hang around with him. And I definitely haven't got a plan on how I am going to bring up what I want from him, or how I'm going to get back to LA.

God, I wish I knew how far and how quickly I could push this. And I wish I knew what I could expect from Jack in return.

The second day with a man is always the hardest. It's like walking on eggshells, trying to read the lay of the land and being careful not to overstep and get booted to the door, all while managing to remain easygoing and entertaining.

Who are you kidding, Linda? You never have an easy time with men, second day or any day.

You'd think after all of the musicians I've been with, I'd know how to do this better. But I don't. My relationships with men always start with bed and end with a brush-off. I can't seem to get it right, no matter how many men I'm with.

Jack is far from my first random-encounter-morning-after with a stranger. But oh, he is definitely my highest stakes game yet.

He is the kind of man a foolish groupie falls in love with. The total rock star package: handsome, charming, intelligent, brilliant, and nice. The most dangerous kind of encounter. The kind where you wake up one morning completely delusional and lying to yourself that there might be a way to keep him.

My eyes run the line of his jaw, down his tan neck which disappears into a loose, pale-pink cotton shirt. Everything about him—from the softly faded jeans, to the flip-flops, the lightly mussed golden hair tucked beneath an LA Lakers cap—is ordinary and extraordinary at once.

As if he senses me studying him, his fingers do a fast squeeze of mine, and he moves my hand to rest on his thigh before he has to shift the car again.

I turn my head so I can focus on the homes.

"How long have you lived here?" I ask.

"My entire life. I was born and raised in that house."

My brows lift. "Really? I can't imagine getting to live in one house my entire life. Doris and I moved almost every year until I was in high school and she bought the condo."

"Where in LA are you from?"

I shrug and make a face. "Reseda."

He smiles, but doesn't remark. Reseda tells him as much about me as seeing this tells me about him.

"And your family?" he asks.

"Just my mom and me."

"What does Doris do?" he asks.

I flush. I don't like answering questions about myself. All of us don't come from stucco-wall, iron-gate, picture-pretty lives.

I feel his stare. It doesn't lessen on me. Reluctantly, I say, "She's a waitress in Encino."

I pick up a box of tapes from the floorboard beneath me, open the case, and pretend to focus on them. I look up just as we pass beneath a high metal arch with a bar that proudly proclaims:

Hope Ranch.

Appropriately named neighborhood, I think sarcastically to myself. Our condo complex is called Meadow View, except there isn't a meadow to view within a hundred miles of the place. That's appropriate, as well.

I continue to run my thumb along the tops of the tapes, reading the labels.

"And your dad?" he asks, rolling to a stop at a red light.

I shrug. "I don't know and I don't want to talk about it."

Crap. Good one, Linda. There was my opening to ask if Jack knows my dad and I slammed it shut without thinking.

He eases into the corner where the seat meets the door, in an angle better to face me, and fixes his gaze on me intently.

"What about a boyfriend? A girl as stunning as you surely has a boyfriend."

"I don't want to talk about him, either."

Jack laughs, settles back into his seat, puts the car in gear and I realize that the light has turned green.

"Guys giving you a bit of trouble, are they?"

I give a pert, saucy nod.

"Nothing but." I change the subject. "I can't believe you have the Sex Pistols and the Motels in here. Christ, there's even Romeo Void."

Jack laughs and frowns simultaneously. "Why shouldn't I have them?"

I shrug. "I don't know. I just expected something different from you."

I lift my gaze back up to find him smiling at me.

He picks up my hand and places a light kiss on the tips of my fingers.

"I'm a pretty basic kind of guy, Linda. You remember that and we'll get along just fine."

We will, will we? I take my lower lip into my teeth and give it a gentle nip to hold back my smile.

"Who says I want to get along with you?" I taunt teasingly.

His gaze touches mine. "Your eyes."

He hits the turn signal, pulls into a parking lot, and I suddenly lose awareness of my surroundings.

"You are trying very hard to make me like you. The question is why?"

He parks the car in a space, turns off the ignition and leans into me, one hand still on the steering wheel.

"You need to ask why?" I counter flippantly.

His gaze sharpens on my face.

"It feels like you want something from me and are afraid to ask. I just can't figure out what. But I'm certain you want something."

Fuck, how does he know that? Have I become *that* obvious?

I rally a mischievous expression. "Maybe I just want your hot body."

Jack shakes his head in frustration. He climbs from the car and is around to my door before I can slow down my racing heartbeat.

He's on to me and I don't have a clue what I should do here. Should I throw my cards up on the table and risk him showing me the door, or be patient until he's more into me, more willing to do me a favor?

I don't have a good enough feel for the man to be know what his reaction will be if I ask him to help me find my father. And I definitely don't want to blow what may be my only real chance of locating him.

Jack can do with a phone call what I could never do in a lifetime: find a high-demand studio musician who hops around the world recording drum tracks. I've been hunting Brian Cray for three years and I haven't even been able to discover where he lives yet.

He opens the car door for me and that adds to the weirdness of being here with him. It's not something I'm comfortable with or used to or expect from him.

I climb out of the car and stand beside Jack. He closes my door and plants his hands against it on either side of me. I'm suddenly surrounded by the feel, the scent, and the warmth of him. The lock of his eyes is burning and intense. My heart jumps into my throat and begins to beat there.

"It's completely unnecessary, you know," he whispers.

My eyes widen. "Excuse me? I don't understand. What's unnecessary?"

"Trying hard to make me like you."

Before I know it, he's got me flattened against the car door, pinning me against it with his hips and his lips are on mine. It happened so fast that I can't stop my body from reacting. I moan into his mouth, my lips part and his tongue instantly takes advantage of my scattered senses. His hands slip between me and the metal, cupping my backside to bring me flush against what is definitely a fully engaged male.

"I already like you, so stop trying so hard, and let's just enjoy each other," he murmurs, and with that he releases my body and steps back.

I stare up at him. In the blink of an eye, he's calm, smiling Jack again.

"Do you want to pick the store or should I?" he asks, taking my fingers in his and leading me across the asphalt.

I shrug, unable to speak. My heart rate is through the roof. My skin feels like it's got a flash sunburn. I'm more than a little frightened, though I'm not sure of what. From the corner of his eyes, Jack is watching every expression flitter across my face as though he were unaffected by our outburst of passion and is playing some sort of game with me.

But what game could he want to play with me? Linda Cray from Reseda isn't even sport for him.

CHAPTER SIX

Jack guides me through the outdoor mall, amid heavy stares. He stops at the entrance of a pricey, upscale boutique and he doesn't even seem aware of the dozens of people gawking at him.

He smiles. "What do you think? Do you think you might find something you like in here?"

My gaze shifts to the elegantly dressed mannequins in the front windows.

"Sure. What's not to love? But really, I don't need anything. The housekeeper's jeans and t-shirts are just fine with me. I can wash them and return them when I'm back in LA."

Shaking his head, Jack pulls open the door. "You're the kind of girl a man wants to treat well and a very difficult girl *to* treat well. You might want to rethink that, Linda. You need to learn to let a man be good to you."

He says that with a heavy air of frustration, but his magnificent blue eyes are twinkling.

I arch a brow. "Thanks for the advice. I'll keep that in mind if a man ever takes me shopping again."

He brushes a thumb along my chin and kisses my lips. "Oh, they will. I'm surprised some man hasn't snatched you up already."

"Nope. Not even a nibble."

"Amazing."

With his hand on the small of my back, he guides me before him into the softly lit store. Above the cash register counter in intricate, swirling pink letters: Back Street.

Well, that's exactly the kind of place a man like him should take a girl like me. Back street store for your back street girl. Everything in here is either black or pink. The black is fine, but the pink makes me want to vomit.

"My daughter likes this store. You should be able to find something here."

My head tilts to the side as I stare at him. His daughter? She's couldn't be more than ten if that picture in his bedroom is recent.

I peek at the tag of a cute black V-neck cashmere sweater. Seven hundred dollars. The man buys seven hundred dollar sweaters for a ten year old.

I smile. "Everything is beautiful in here, but really…"

He stops me with a finger across my lips. "Shush. Let me do this. Stop fighting everything. You don't have to fight anything with me."

He starts to lightly brush my lip as if in warning not to speak, and I'm instantly claimed by a flashing want to do so much more than speak. Without effort, his touch sends the feel of him all through my body.

God, he's so hot, I think, and step back from him.

Jack starts to wander the store in easy grace as if it's perfectly normal for him to be here and to be with me.

Fine. We'll have it his way. I'll shop.

At a rack, I start to jerk the hangers one by one away from me. Most of it is too Beverly Hills. I like dark colors, simple lines, and outfits that are versatile. Jeanette thinks my fashion style is morose and Doris buys me a pink sweater every birthday.

I shove a dozen outfits on hangers to whiz away, rejected. I pause. Have I finally hit pay dirt? This is kind of cute. I pull out a simple sundress in black and hold it up in front of me.

From the corner of my eye, I note the saleswoman standing in the dressing room doorway watching me. She is thirtyish, blond, pretty and tanned, impeccably turned out in designer jumpsuit and some really stunning platforms shoes I wish I owned. She looks more like a cover girl than a shop girl.

I search with my gaze to see if they carry shoes in the store. They do. Lucky me. I'll be even luckier if they carry the ones she's wearing. As ashamed as I am to realize it, I can swallow my pride enough to accept Jack's generosity if it means walking out of here with a pair of shoes like those.

I glance at her and smile. "Do you sell here the shoes you're wearing?"

She makes a slight nod. She does not return my smile. My cheeks turn icy cool, even with the blush I can feel covering them.

Damn, she's watching me like a hawk because she's wondering if I'm a shoplifter.

I turn to spot Jack across the store, looking thoughtful, browsing intensely—of all things—lingerie. Maybe he has some inner freak in him. I haven't seen it yet, but that doesn't mean it isn't there.

I start to laugh. With the black sundress in hand, I cross the store to him as snooty girl's nose moves with me.

Jack looks up. "Did you find something you think might work?"

I nod. "A dress." My eyes shift to the panties drawer he has opened. "Are you finding something that works for *you*?"

Before he can respond, across the room sounds: "Jack! Jack Parker."

We both turn at the same time to see the saleswoman closing in on us.

"Patty," Jack's husky voice responds in pleasure.

He pulls her against him in a friendly embrace and they are both smiling in a way that makes me taut with unexpected curiosity.

"I feel so embarrassed," she purrs, lightly tapping his chest with a manicured nail. "I've been in back checking stock all morning. Somehow I didn't see you come in."

Her gaze hits me and bounces away to quickly scan the store.

"Is Chrissie with you?"

"She's east with Walter for two weeks. The house is miserably quiet without her. I even miss having Rene underfoot."

Patty tilts her head slightly to the side and gives Jack a reproachful look. "Rene is a handful, but you adore my daughter, admit it. Every inch as charming as her mother."

They both laugh and Patty finally takes a step back from him.

"You haven't stopped over in a while. I've been worried about you. Are you OK?"

Jack says that softly in a way that tells me this isn't a casual question.

Patty nods and almost looks like she's dabbing at an imaginary tear. "The divorce has been hard on Rene, but we're both getting through it."

"If you need anything, Patty, just ask."

She smiles and touches at another fake tear.

"It's good to see you out, Jack," she says, this time her voice quieter and more thoughtful. "It's been a long time since you've wandered out this way. What brings you here today? Anything I can help you find?"

Jack turns to me, stunning smile in place, and casually slips an arm around my waist.

"This is Linda." He says my name in a smooth kind of way that doesn't suggest a need or invitation for inquiry. "She landed in Santa Barbara without her luggage. She needs everything."

Patty shifts her eyes to me. She sizes me up in a head-to-toe, fast-moving glance. I size her up. We lock gazes. Aha. We're instant enemies.

"This is Patty Thompson," Jack continues, as if oblivious to the female tension surrounding him. "I've known her since kindergarten. She's my neighbor on the left. The hideous two-story modern structure that blocks out the view for the rest of the neighborhood."

Patty laughs and rolls her eyes. "You can't still be angry about that."

Jack's smile is charming. "You should never have built up, Patty. No one owns the view. But you're forgiven. It was probably George's idea anyway."

She colors prettily and her smile is cleverly neutral in a way that tells me that building that monstrous house was very much her idea.

"You can't take a thing he says seriously," she explains, "or you'll never speak to him again. Would you like me to start a room for you, Miss...?"

Aha. So she wants to know who I am. Whatever Pretty Patty is about, I'm not playing. My last name is not a card I'm ready to lay face up with Jack.

I shove my hanger at her. "If you could start a dressing room that would be great."

Her eyes widen just a tad, then she smiles again at Jack, and slithers off toward the back of the store.

"Interesting neighbor," I comment, leaning against the lingerie drawers.

"She's not so bad. She's a very good friend. She'll grow on you."

I smile. I wouldn't count on it, Jack, not even if I'm here a hundred years instead of the handful of days I expect this adventure to be.

He lifts up a stunning black shift with little beaded pearls on the bodice and matching robe.

"You would look wonderful in this. What do you think?"

I arch a brow. "You pick. You probably have more experiencing buying high-end lingerie than me."

Something flashes in his eyes too quickly for me to catch and then is quickly tucked behind that famous Jackson Parker smile.

He sets the silk back on its hook and turns to study another nightgown.

After a moment of silence, he says, "Actually, I don't. I've never taken a woman shopping before."

Those piercing blue eyes fix on me, powerfully making the heat immediately rise to cheeks.

"I'm not a womanizer," he adds softly. "I don't do things like last night. I don't sleep around. I'm a one woman at a time kind of guy."

I flush again.

There's a lot in that statement: it's part reprimand to make sure I know I insulted him; part warning, like he doesn't want me to get too serious about us; and part heart-meltingly adorable in how he says "one woman kind of guy."

I need to defuse this. But how? I need to get this all light and happy-go-lucky again. I suck in a breath.

"Really? What a shame. I was going to ask you to come into the dressing room with me for a fast fuck, but I'd be the only one who knows how to do it."

My lips close in on him and I take his mouth in a fully open, tongue invading, impossible to mistake kind of kiss.

I leave him quickly, heading toward the watching Patty, my dressing room, and my little black sundress.

I peek at him over my shoulder and find him smiling again.

Patty directs me to a dressing room and I step in.

"You're a size four, right?"

My eyes widen just a tad. I nod.

"Why don't you let me pick out an assortment of things for you, Linda? You looked a little lost out there trying to figure out how to assemble a wardrobe. I don't know how long you'll be in town, but if your luggage doesn't arrive you'll definitely need more than one dress."

Oh, rudeness uncapped now that we are alone!

"Pick away," I say frivolously, tossing my Lakers cap on the bench. With my fingers, I shake out my curls as Patty closes the dressing room door.

I toss my flip-flops into a corner and pull off Maria's jeans and t-shirt. I take the dress from the hanger, jerk it over my head, and zip up the back.

Smoothing the garment over my lean curves, I turn toward the mirror. I stare at myself in surprise. The simple black dress is so elegant put on. Somehow, it makes me look completely different, and no longer like a fish out of water in this posh, casually trendy coastal town.

I struggle to pull the tag from the back to see it in the mirror. *Crap.* Nine hundred seventy-five dollars for a tiny square of linen cut into an Audrey Hepburn A-line dress!

It makes me nervous just having the darn thing on me. I'm about to pull it off when I hear a knock and Patty barges in without asking if she can enter.

She freezes halfway into the room. "Oh god. I didn't see it with the hat and glasses on."

"Excuse me?"

Patty turns me towards the mirror again. "Dark curls. Dark eyes and wearing that dress. You look like Lena. I was wondering why he's running around with someone like you."

My insides grow cold. Running around with someone like me? The ways she says that makes it pointedly catty.

Her eyes do another fast once over of my form. It is done in a very uncomplimentary way.

"Jack always did like a girl that was just a smidge exotic."

In some sort of masterful, rich woman manner, she manages to make the word *exotic* sound like a pejorative.

"I'm not exotic. I'm Jewish. Or is that considered exotic here?"

Patty reddens, turns, and deposits on the hooks the

mountain of garments she came in with.

"I brought you a little bit of everything you might need," she says.

I smile without saying thank you and wait for her to leave.

Forty minutes later, there is a pile of clothing and shoes on the floor, and I'm sitting on the bench wondering what I should do about this. I can't let Jack buy me all this. Patty's comments have pricked at me since she said them.

By the end of trying on garments, I'm feeling miserable, slimy and opportunistic. Am I shamefully taking advantage of a man drowning in sadness and loss? I don't know for sure and that bothers the hell out of me.

Usually the game is casual sex, a few laughs, and nothing more. That's my relationship MO, and if I learn some tidbit of information about my father along the way, I consider that fair trade.

This thing with Jack is something I haven't experienced before. Something different than any of my other affairs have been. Two days, and I already have feelings for him when I never allow myself to feel anything for any man. But Jackson Parker is a special kind of man, unlike any man I've ever met.

I'm out of my comfort zone, I don't know how to handle him, I don't know how to control myself, and I haven't got a clue where this is going.

CHAPTER SEVEN

We are quiet on the drive from the mall up State Street. We both seem lost in our thoughts. I haven't a clue what's bothering Jack. I know what's bothering me.

I can't shake my feelings of dishonesty in what I'm doing here with him. It has only intensified after seeing what a tiny wardrobe at a fashionable Santa Barbara boutique costs, and watching as he paid for it.

It's the closest I've ever come to taking money from a man and I don't like it. That I am only staying because I want something from him makes accepting his kindness all the more despicable.

I peek over at him and smile. My smile is not returned. My already tense muscles grow more taught with apprehension.

The vibe in the car is strange. Something has changed in him. It started after the dressing room, when I rejoined him in the store. The smile left his face and I haven't seen it since. Without batting an eye, he paid for everything, took the bags and put them in the trunk. But he hasn't smiled at me since.

He isn't talking and he's maintaining a careful distance between us. I wonder if Pretty Patty put poison in his ears while I was conveniently out of the way trying on dresses.

I stare down at my hands and knot my fingers. I feel very shaky, like I do right before something terrible comes my way. I am an expert at sensing impending doom. Whatever is happening, isn't going to be good for me.

I look up at him. The tension is unbearable.

"Do you think you can arrange for me to get back to LA? I don't know how to catch up with my ride. I don't know if she's still in Santa Barbara. I have class next week."

He downshifts the car and turns on the signal. "When do you want to go?"

My heart leaps into my mouth and I suddenly feel emotional. Why did I ask that? Why did I push instead of waiting for his mood to pass? We've gone from "stay as long as you want" to "when do you want to go."

I stare back down at my hands. "I have to be back by Wednesday. The school monitors my attendance because of my scholarship."

His expression hardens. "I can arrange for a car and a driver. It's no big deal."

Oh no. He wants me to leave. What's changed? His jaw is clenching and his eyes are fixed on the road.

I can't stand the tension. It makes me attack.

"I can leave tonight if you want me to," I say stiffly.

I lift my chin and wait.

"There is no need to make a decision this second," he says patiently.

I look away from him, searching for something to say. I

realize we've stopped and are parked in a lot close to a small restaurant with white and blue trim. Philadelphia House. It looks fancy.

I'm glad I wore the black Audrey Hepburn A-line dress and the new platform shoes when I left the dressing room. I don't think the housekeeper's clothes would quite work here.

"I thought you might be hungry," he murmurs, opening his door.

I nod. It's nearly sunset. I'm not hungry, but anything that postpones the discussion of sending me on my way is a good thing.

I watch him move around the car to my door, drinking in the sight of him. To think last night, after hours of fiery sex, I slept naked and sweaty in his arms until morning. It makes his change of demeanor all the more perplexing.

I wait in silence as he opens my door. I peek at him through my lashes as I climb from my seat, and pause to smooth down the dress over my curves. Even as tight as it is, it bunched up in my seat and, darn, the lap belt left a slight crease in the linen.

I feel his eyes follow my hands as he waits for me to finish preening. Suddenly, for some reason, the atmosphere between us changes and there is an electric charge between us that I can read without effort.

When his eyes meet mine they are a deep glittering blue. My breathing alters as the tick in his cheek twitches. The soft muscles against my new silk panties frantically start to pulse.

Oh my god, he's not angry. He's turned on. He is totally into me and I told him I wanted to leave.

I bite my lip and his eyes darken.

"You don't have a clue what you do to me, do you, Linda?"

he says simply.

My heartbeat picks up and I am instantly hot everywhere. The tension in the car was sexual! He's hot for me again, and, like a switch he flipped, I'm startled to realize I am immediately hot for him, too. I drink in the perfect lines of his face, slightly tight with desire. I want him. Here. Now. Someway.

"Why don't you show me," I whisper.

My fingers close around his shirt and I pull his body into me as I claim his mouth. The joining of our lips is hungry at first touch, and instantly he has my face in a vice-like grip, his tongue expertly exploring my mouth, his body pinning me against the car door. His erection is digging into me, straining against his jeans.

I'm back on familiar ground. I know how to fix my earlier blunder and what my next move should be.

I rub my body against his erection, I feel a twitch in response, and I drag my lips back, breathing heavily against his mouth because I've gone from zero to sixty in record time again. I rapidly take in oxygen to steady myself.

"I'm going to the bathroom. I'm leaving the door unlocked. Get a table and meet me there."

I don't wait for an answer. Quickly, I move ahead of him into the restaurant. If there is a God in heaven, the bathroom will be empty. I am dripping and wet, frantic and horny, and all Jack did was kiss me as I rubbed against his erection.

The hostess smiles at me as I step into the dimly lit entrance and, after an abrupt inquiry over where the restrooms are, I bypass the dining room and hurry down a long, narrow corridor.

I turn the knob and thankfully find it unlocked. I slip into the room. I plant my hands on the vanity, breathing heavily. I wasn't even thinking about sex in the car and now I'm desperate for him.

I look up, catching my reflection in the mirror. There is a wildness I've never seen before in my eyes. A passion flush on my cheeks, and a rapid rise and fall to my achy breasts.

What if he doesn't follow?

I chase away the thought. If Jack is half as turned on as I am, he'll follow.

My gaze flitters around the room. It's large, carpeted and beautifully decorated. There is even a chaise before a full wall mirror. A well-appointed fuck parlor in every way.

The door opens and I whirl to see Jack enter. He clicks the lock in place behind him.

"Now that you have me here, what are you going to do with me?" Jack whispers, traces of humor and lust on the gorgeous angles of his face.

I suck in hard. I feel so powerful when he looks at me that way. I am beyond excited, yet I can't will my legs to take me from my side of the room to his.

He starts to unbutton his jeans, those potent blue eyes never leaving mine.

"Not so bold now, are you?" he asks.

His jeans are hanging low on his hips as he kicks off his shoes. Just watching him is like a mini orgasm, and he is calmly undressing and waiting for me to make the first move.

"I can't hold back forever," he warns, as he takes away the space between us. "But you are in charge, baby. You got me here, now take me."

Oh my! This time he's all mine to play with, and it has just kicked up my arousal to the temperature of the sun's surface. There's none of that *Be patient, Linda,* no savoring of the senses from Jack. He's out of his mind, burning hot, just like me. And this time, he wants me to fuck him.

His pants drop to the floor and thought is no longer necessary. I meld my body into his and he returns my kiss with a passion that matches my own. My scattered senses are only vaguely aware of my movement toward the chaise and the swift removal of my clothing.

I want him so badly that I'm not even conscious of how we end up with him lying on the chaise and me riding him. My breathing catches as I swallow his flesh, rush and ride him. My need for release is blinding.

I groan as he tilts his hips up to meet my motions, filling me so deeply that my head begins to roll in agonizing pleasure. I feel his lips and hands all over my body. My hardened nipples. The sensitive flesh of my ears. The underside of my jaw and smooth surface of my neck.

I have no idea what I'm doing. The feel of him radiates through my limbs. His breathing is hard, matching mine, his pelvis taking over to drive the rhythm. His face is taut with anticipation and want, and it feels so good, this brutal chase beneath me that I control.

I plant my hands on his shoulders, still my hips and stop the race. His eyes open and I gently roll my hips, stroking up, then slowly downward. A fast lift and then a brutal swallowing. I start to increase the pace again. The feel of him makes me desperate with want.

His head rolls on the chaise and his eyes close.

I watch him.

I am fucking him and he's savoring it like a man who hasn't had this in a very long time.

~~~

We are sweaty and hot, curled into each other, lying on the chaise. Jack is smoking a cigarette. In the frenzy of shedding our clothes, Jack ended up with his shirt on and nothing below the waist. The image of him damp half-dressed and damp with passion makes me giggle.

I bury my face against his chest, then peek up at him sheepishly. I'm sure that my eyes are still glowing wickedly.

"We have a problem," I whisper.

"We don't have a problem in the world, baby."

I laugh.

I stare at him with round eyes.

"We've been in here a long time. It's a tiny restaurant. I don't know how I go to our table without being totally embarrassed."

Jack pretends to give it thought. The smile in his eyes make them gleam. "We don't," he concedes. "There's a door at the end of the hallway. We can ditch our table and go next door and eat."

I arch a brow in playful suspicion. "Aha. And how would you know that? Have you done this before?"

He tucks a hair behind my ear and shakes his head. "No. This was a novelty for me. I've never done this before."

He smiles.

My eyes grow large in surprise. "Are you saying not in this restaurant or are you saying you've never been out with a woman and snuck off for a quickie in an opportunistic place before?"

"No, I have not done the quickie thing." He shakes his head and frowns as if recalling something uncomfortably. "I married Lena at twenty." He starts to trace the lines of my face with an index finger. "This was not her type of thing."

I make a face. "What? Having sex?"

He smiles and taps me on the nose.

"Spontaneity." He turns to me and brushes the curls off my face. "You are completely unexpected, but I'd be a liar if I said I wasn't having fun with you, Linda. I can't remember the last time I had fun doing anything."

The look in his eyes makes my heart drop to my knees and then take off, beating fiercely. That is far from a casual comment. His voice is earnest and tender and peaceful.

I kiss him on the cheek. "I have fun with you, too. I particularly had fun with you a few minutes ago."

I nibble lightly on his neck.

"Always a wisecrack." Laughing, he sits up and rakes a hand through his sex-mussed waves. "Enough. We need to plot how to get out of here."

In between searing kisses and caresses, we take our clothes from the floor and dress. I pause at the mirror and try to smooth the *just been fucked* look of my curls.

Over top of me, in the reflection, Jack is smoothing his hair, too. His fingers combing through his hair makes me think of how those same fingers have expertly caressed my body.

I flush and smile at him in the mirror.

"Am I presentable?" he asks, amused with himself and clearly still amused by me.

I shake my head and laugh.

Jack's efforts were pointless. His bright golden waves always have the look of *just been fucked* hair. I doesn't help that his shirt is buttoned crookedly.

I kiss him on the underside of his jaw, bite my lip to hold

back my laughter, take his hand and pull him from the bathroom.

As we move down the hallway, I peek over my shoulder to see if we're being watched and then look to find Jack watching me with the strangest expression on his face.

Our careful trek down the hallway, for some reason, feels sillier with each step. I am laughing uproariously by the time we reach the dimly lit parking lot.

Jack wags a finger at me. "You are not the least bit subtle or clever."

"There is no point being subtle or clever. You look like a man who just got laid in the ladies' room." I bend over with laughter. "How the hell did your shirt get buttoned crooked when you didn't take off the damn thing?"

He looks down, looks at me, and the look in eyes makes me dart away from him. With three graceful strides he catches me, and we are laughing harder, stumbling, kissing, and hugging without reason.

"You could have told me that before we left," he growls playfully, pressing his forehead into mine, smiling.

I make a small pout as he unbuttons and re-buttons his shirt.

I sigh heavily. "Now what? We can't go back in there and I'm starving."

Jack points at a rustic wood structure across the parking lot. Creekside Tavern.

"How about there? They have very good food, and from the looks of the crowd they're going to have live music tonight."

From elegant eatery to biker pub. But having him in the bathroom just now was definitely worth the downgrade.

I laugh. "Sure, why not?"

He takes my hand. I stare at his fingers curled around mine, as he guides me toward the restaurant. He opens the front door, and a rush of warm air and noise hits me as I step in before him.

The décor is appropriately rustic to match the exterior. The ceiling is high, with open log beams, and the floor is painted concrete. On one side of the room there is a giant stone fireplace and on the other are pool tables. Everything is in one giant, open space: the dance floor and stage; the bar and cocktail tables; and the tables for dining.

It's packed, and every set of eyes in the joint, in varying levels of obviousness, are fixed on Jack.

A man rushes across the room, hand outstretched. "Jack. Good to see you. God, what's it been? A year?"

Jack laughs. "At least a year. Great to see you, Rusty. Do you think you could get us a table? You look pretty busy here."

Rusty reaches over a counter for some menus. "I always have a table for you, and you know that. Come on. Let's get you seated."

We are led to a corner table in a discreet location.

Jack pulls back my chair and I sink into it.

"What can I get the two of you to drink?" Rusty asks.

"I'll have the usual, and bring Linda—" Jack pauses thoughtfully and laughs. "What do you want? I don't know what you drink."

Oh crap. Nothing says *just picked-up girl* like not knowing what she drinks. I can feel the owner's eyes hone in on me with curiosity.

I flush from chin to hairline. "Whatever Jack's having, I'll have the same."

Jack smiles. "You don't have to not drink because of me."

I flush even darker. "I'm not. I don't drink very much."

Crap. I just made what I am more obvious. I grab my napkin and focus on putting it across my lap.

Rusty pats Jack on the back. "Two sparkling waters with lime, then. The waitress will be right over, Jack. Enjoy your evening."

I open my menu.

He leans into the table. "What?"

When I peek over the top, Jack frowns.

"Did you have to make is so obvious that I'm just some piece of ass you're hanging around with?" I whisper furiously.

Startled, he eases back into his chair. "You've lost me."

My eyes round. "You asked me what I wanted to drink."

Now he looks perplexed. "OK. And you're pissed off at that because…?"

"Because telling him you don't know what I drink tells him I am—"

I was about to say *just some girl you picked up*, but that's what I am, so why the heck do I feel the need to say it.

I bury my nose back into my menu.

Jack is silent. I can feel him watching me.

I don't look at him. "What do you recommend here?"

"Linda…" His voice is like a caress. "…look at me."

"It's all good. It's OK with me that we have some fun and a few laughs. Just don't ever treat me like a piece of ass and we'll get along just fine."

"I would never do that," he counters forcefully.

"You just did," I whisper.

He shakes his head. "I don't know where you get these ideas you have about things. I merely asked you what you want to drink."

I nod.

"Linda, look at me."

I exhale a ragged breath and come out from behind my menu.

"I've already told you I consider us friends."

He reaches across the table, he takes my hand and places a searing kiss in my palm.

He keeps hold of my fingers to lightly rub them against his lips.

"There is only one of us who thinks you're a tough, roll-with-the-fun girl, and it isn't me. You're an amazing woman. I am happy that I've met you."

I don't know what to say. I don't know if he is changing the level of our relationship or just being charming or just making an observation.

He soothes my hand on the table and covers it with his. "Do you know what you'd like to order?"

I look up, startled, to find the waitress standing above us. By the flush on her cheeks and the way she peeks at us from under her long bangs, I can tell she witnessed that whole scene and thinks something thrillingly romantic just happened here.

I stare at Jack, unable to articulate anything, and whatever is in my expression makes the smile slip from his face.

"Why don't you give us a minute," he says to the waitress.

The second we're alone, I pounce.

"Don't play games with me by pretending you want this to go somewhere, when we both know that isn't true. That is an unkind thing to do to a girl." My voice is soft.

The expression in his eyes tells me I've offended him again.

"That's not the response I expected," he says, after a long

pause.

"Enlighten me, then. What did you expect me to say after a douse of your charming bullshit?" And because I can't stop the knee-jerk reaction, I add "Thank you?"

Silence.

"To tell you the truth, I don't have the slightest idea. I say what I feel, Linda. I don't think about what's next."

We stare at each other. Instead of getting all male and hotheaded over my snappiness, he just sits there quietly trying to make sense of me.

Jeez, why doesn't Jack ever behave in a way that I know how to deal with?

"I don't know what to make of you," I say, with a slight shake of my head.

"Then we're even. There are times I don't know what to make of you either." His eyes study me in such a puzzled way. "Are we still fighting or are we friends again?"

His golden brow puckers in an absolutely adorable way.

I start to laugh.

Jack frowns. "Why are you laughing?"

"We're an interesting couple."

Jack relaxes his elbows on the table and his smile is spellbinding. "You're coming along, Linda. You are starting to show progress."

He leans across the table and kisses me on the mouth, in a manner that ends this awkwardness for us both.

When the waitress returns, we are both smiling and laughing.

Jack orders dinner for us both, since I can't even think of food with his blue eyes smiling at me the way they are, and two hours pass as we chat and linger over Steak Diane and a glass of local Pinot Noir for me.

I am completely relaxed and content by the time we finish our meal.

"Are you ready to go?" he asks.

It's still early, the first band is on stage readying for their set, and I'm surprised he wants to leave before the music begins.

"You don't want to stay for a while? I've never been in a biker bar before."

Jack chuckles. "If you want to find good live music in a strange town, go where the Harleys are lined up at the front door."

I crinkle my nose. "Not really?"

"Really." Jack tosses his napkin on the table. "And no I don't want to stay." His gaze roams over me in a leisurely way, impossible to mistake. "I'd rather be somewhere more private with you."

"A man after my own heart," I whisper, stealing one of his phrases.

He motions for the waitress and asks for the check.

"Just let me pop into the little girl's room."

"Don't be long," he whispers before his lips move urgently against my lips.

Everything is wonderful again.

I smile as I walk away from the table.

There's a line at the bathroom, and I lean against the wall feeling sexy and loose and ready for him.

I still can't get my head around the fact that I'm with him, but it's definitely been one terrific ride and I am eager for more. And I'm going to get more because Jackson Parker is taking Linda Cray home to bed.

I blush and giggle.

My cheeks hurt from smiling as I push off the wall when the bathroom door opens.

I'm about to step in when a harsh hand latches on my arm and pulls me away.

"What the fuck do you think you're doing taking off on me?"

Oh crap. Rob. I shake my arm out of his hold and step back.

I stare up at him. "You looked busy at the party so I left. Now if you'll excuse me I have a date waiting."

He grabs my arm again. "Date? Who the fuck would date you?"

I slap him so hard on the face my hand burns. I hurry down the hallway away from him.

"Get back here, Linda," I hear him growl behind me.

Shit, he's following me.

"Don't you fucking walk away from me!"

Why does he always have to be so loud and obnoxious? I can feel people staring at me as I cut a path through the bar patrons.

Jack is still sitting at the table when I get there. I fix my eyes on him.

"Can we leave, please? Now."

Jack looks up startled. He rises from his chair. "What's wrong?"

"I need to get out of here. Fast."

Jack takes my hand and starts escorting me through the tables.

From behind us: "Hey buddy, that's my girlfriend you're trying to leave with."

Jack turns on a dime, somehow putting me behind him, with his body between me and Rob.

"I'm not your buddy," Jack says in an even tone that's more intimidating than if his voice had been raised. "If you so much as speak to Linda again, it will be the last thing you ever do."

I don't know what's got Rob more stumped: the warning or that it came from Jackson Parker.

"If you walk out that door, I'm not taking you back this time, Linda." Rob's eyes lock on me with burning fury. "Feeling like the groupie *Queen for a day*, are you? We both know you'll be back when he's done with you, just like after that guitarist in Hollywood and the drummer in Venice and…"

Unexpectedly, Rusty the owner grabs me by the arm and yanks me away from Jack. I whirl back just as Jack's fist makes contact with Rob's jaw, causing an ominous cracking sound, and then Rob flies back landing sprawled on the floor.

It all happens so fast it doesn't seem real.

"I warned you," Jack says. "Stay down. Stay away from her."

CHAPTER EIGHT

As we drive back to the house, Jack is silent, flexing his cut and bloodied hand.

Five minutes. Not a word out of him since we left the restaurant. I'm more than a little anxious and terrified of what's going to come next.

It was an ugly scene. People gawking. It will probably make the papers. Jack has got to be pissed and he's got to hate me.

Rob specializes in ugly scenes and let loose my fucked up lifestyle for all the world to hear.

Cautiously, I look at Jack from the corner of my eye. Jeez, why doesn't he just let it out and get it over with. The waiting is unbearable.

"Boyfriend?"

His quiet voice makes me jump. "He was never my friend."

Jack shakes his head. "Why the fuck would you be with someone like that?"

I feel tears burn in my eyes and I fight them back. "I don't know. I can't explain it. It's just one of those foolish things girls do sometimes. Wrong guy but convenient."

"And the rest of the shit he spewed?"

I flinch. I don't need Jack to explain what he's asking about. I can see it in his eyes.

"It's complicated. OK?"

He hits the turn signal.

"Everything about you is complicated. It's part of the turn-on and part of the risk."

He parks the car, opens his door and I spring out of mine before he can come around the car to open it.

Silently, I follow behind him as he enters the house. He heads straight for the kitchen, turns on a light, and starts rummaging in a cabinet.

I hang back in the doorway, watching. "You should wash your hand. You're bleeding."

He slaps a first aid kit down beside the sink and turns on the water. He starts carefully washing his hand and I can tell by his expression it hurts.

Another handful of minutes drag by in silence.

He looks over his shoulder at me. "I haven't been in a fight in fifteen years."

His tone is carefully neutral.

"It wasn't much of a fight, if you ask me."

I see his back shimmy with a reluctant laugh. I wonder if the laugh means he's thawing a bit.

"Should we go to a hospital? Do you think you broke anything? We should really get that checked."

"No. Just a cut. Nothing broken. It's fine."

I nearly collapse in relief. I am so lost in the beauty of who Jack is that there are times I forget *who* Jack is: one of the world's greatest guitarists.

Christ, if he had ruined his hand because of me I could never forgive myself.

He pulls from the drawer a clean kitchen towel and I cross the room to him then. I reach for the first aid kit and he stops me.

"No, I'll do it," he says, taking the kit with him to the island and sinking down on a stool.

Feeling guilty, I push his unoffended hand out of the way.

"You can't bandage your own hand. Don't be an ass about this."

He frowns at me, still angry but now just a smidge amused.

I sit on the stool next to him. I take out a square of gauze and dampen it with antiseptic.

I start to carefully dab at his torn flesh and Jack winces.

"How long we're you involved with him?" he asks.

I take a deep breath and try to focus on what I'm doing. I thought we were past questions on this.

"On and off since high school. He's my BTN."

"BTN?"

I reach for another square of gauze. I cut a strip of medical tape and tack it on the counter.

I look up to find his eyes waiting expertly.

"Are you going to tell me or not? What's a BTN?"

I shake my head as I put the gauze over his cut.

"It's just a stupid term girls use. It stands for better than nothing. The guy you hang out with when you don't have a real boyfriend."

He stares at me gravely, but his expression has softened a little more.

"I don't want you ever seeing him again." His tone has changed to soft, sensual.

"I don't think there is much of a chance of that after tonight."

"Good. He's not someone you should be mixed up with."

I meet his gaze directly. "What do you care?"

"I care, Linda."

His eyes darken.

My breath hitches.

I am suddenly too full of my own emotions.

I step into his arms and kiss him on his chest.

"I'm sorry. I'm sorry I ruined our lovely evening. I'm sorry you hurt your hand because of my crazy life. I make everything shitty. Everything a mess..."

He stops me with a kiss and stands up from his stool wearing a predatory, hungry look.

"Don't apologize, Linda. Take me to bed and make up for it."

I wake alone in the bed, shrouded in moonlight. I sit up, rub my eyes, and check the clock. Four a.m. and Jack is no longer in the room.

After we made love, things felt better between us, but there is still something off with Jack. I can't quite put my finger on it, but instinct tells me something is wrong.

I reach for the duvet to wrap around me and then change my mind. I drop to the floor beside the shopping bags and rummage through them for the pretty black silk nightie set that

Jack slipped into the purchases without asking me.

I pull the dainty shift with the beaded bodice over my head, slip into the robe, and then do a fast check of myself in the mirror.

Wow, is that really me? I look so sexy and yet elegant in this.

I pad down the hallway, checking rooms as I pass. Nothing. Maybe his hand is hurting or has started bleeding through the bandage.

I head toward the kitchen.

I flip on a light. No Jack here. The only wing of the house left to search is where Maria and the kids' bedrooms are.

I really don't want to go there. I don't know how he lives in this house, knowing that his son died here. I would have moved the next day.

I'm about to switch off the lights when something on the patio catches my attention. I lean up over the sink and stare out the wall of glass. The lawn lights are on and there he is.

Jack is sitting on the patio staring out at the ocean. There is something in how he looks right now that makes my heart clench. Beautiful. Isolated. Alone.

I slide open the French doors. Jack's raised voice makes me halt one step out onto the patio. I hadn't noticed the speaker phone on the table beside him.

"I don't care what you think, Walter. You are not taking my daughter away."

"She's not doing well, Jack. I don't know why you can't see it. She won't talk about that night. She needs to talk. You need to get her into counseling."

Jack rakes a frustrated hand through his tousled golden waves. "I know my daughter, Walter. When she's ready to talk, she'll let it out. She was very close to her brother. It is not in her interest to force her to relive his death. I won't do that to my girl. We all deal with things differently."

An aggravated sigh. "I don't want to fight you in court. You know that."

"Then stop, Walter. For all our sakes. Stop. Lena wouldn't want this. It needs to stop."

"She's my granddaughter. All I have left. I love her. I'm doing what I think is right."

"I know you love her, Walter. I know this isn't about you and me. I know you want what's best for Chrissie, but taking her to live with you isn't the answer."

A long silence between them.

"Will you at least consider boarding school instead of a private tutor at home?" says the voice through the phone in weary desperation. "It's not good for her to be that isolated. It might help for her to be around other girls."

"I'm not promising anything, but I'll consider it," Jack says stiffly.

"It would be better all around," Walter says.

Jack clicks off the phone.

He glances up at the sky, his unfathomable blue eyes intense, and his expression is unreadable. But he is troubled, very troubled.

He looks so vulnerable sitting there lost in his worries. He is a stunning man. Golden hair, broad shoulders, narrow hips and a tanned, well-muscled abdomen. But it is the emotions that flash in his eyes, never quite completely hidden, that are drawing me too quickly, too deeply into him.

With the smile in his eyes there is always a ghost of sadness, a peaceful soul at war with a tortured one.

"You're a wonderful man," I whisper. "There isn't a court on earth who would take your daughter away from you."

He turns his head to look at me, a flash of surprise as if he'd been totally unaware of my presence, and then a frown flits across his face.

"How would you know? You haven't any idea what kind of father I am. I've made a lot of mistakes, Linda."

I shrug. "Who hasn't? But I know a good man from a bad man. I know a good father from a bad father. There is one thing *I* know, Jackson Parker. It's men."

He pulls me down on the chaise in front of him, easing me back between his thighs as he drops a kiss on my head. It feels good to have his arms tightly wrapped around me, holding onto me in that way men do in crisis.

And I'm doing what I do best. Just being here for troubled men. Being who they need me to be.

"Why don't you come back to bed, Jack?"

"Can we just sit here and wait for the dawn?"

I nod.

He buries his lips in my hair and I settle more comfortably against him.

"I'm so glad I found you," he whispers.

I smile. "Wrong. I found you."

He laughs.

Then I sense another change in his mood, back into sadness.

"Don't go back to LA yet. Without you, I wouldn't be making it through this week half as well as I am."

"You want me to stay?"

"More than you know."

"Then I'll stay. As long as you need me to."

His hurts. His needs. I am the solace he is holding onto in this isolated bubble of brilliance and misery.

I lean forward and kiss his forearm. But this time is different. I'm not staying only for Jack. This time I'm staying for me.

I've crossed the line. I want Jack to be who I need him to be and I desperately wish there was a way never to face the inevitable reality that he *won't be*.

CHAPTER NINE

Day 7...

I hold the wicker basket and bounce off the edge of the table.

"Can we go home now?" I ask, part exasperated and part amused.

Jack looks up, startled. "What? I love Thursday afternoon farmer's market."

I raise my brows.

"Where do you think I get everything we've been eating?" he adds, smiling.

I ease down the vegetable aisle as he moves on to the peppers. He smiles at absolutely everyone. He talks to anyone who approaches him. And he is unaware that the chemistry beneath the tent is super charged by him and that everyone is staring.

I lean into him. "Doesn't it make you feel uncomfortable to have everyone staring at you?" I whisper.

"They are not staring at me. They're staring at you." He

drops a kiss on my mouth. "You look beautiful today."

I flush, though I admit that my trendy black pantsuit and stylish cork and Italian leather platforms are flattering.

I lower my sunglasses to the tip of my nose.

"Do you miss it?"

Jack is focused on rummaging through the onions. I would never have believed this if I wasn't here seeing it. The man does his own shopping.

"Touring," I add, catching his attention. "The music. The fans. Being adored by everyone."

"I'm still adored by everyone," he says in a boyishly teasing way. "I perform. Just not as much as I used to. But my partying on a bus and being months on the road days are behind me. I have responsibilities now and there's only me."

For some inexplicable reason, Jack putting his daughter before everything else makes me hurt. If only my dad had been this kind of man.

I force a smile. "How long is your daughter gone?"

"Chrissie comes back next week. She's driving up from LA with the housekeeper."

He drops two onions into the basket.

I suffer the feeling of time running out and the pressure of reality closing in. The daughter coming back means he won't want me to stay.

Jack frowns. "Are you OK?"

I nod. "Just tired. Do you think we can leave?"

He takes my hand. "We've pretty much got everything we need this week. Let's get out of here."

I'm silent as we go back to the car. I open the door myself as he settles the basket behind the seat and I snap my seat belt into place.

I stare out the window as we drive up the streets that are starting to become familiar to me. We have settled into a routine of living together that is deceptively comfortable. I'm running out of time. The daughter is returning. I need to ask him if he'll help me find my dad.

"Do you want to stop on the pier for a drink before we head back to the house?" he asks.

"No. I just want to go home."

Home. I've lost perspective so quickly. I shake my head. Get on with it, Linda. Do it!

I turn to angle my body in my seat so I am facing Jack.

"Do you know a drummer name Brian Cray?"

Jack laughs. "That's a name you don't hear very often in the real world. Of course I know him. Everyone in the industry knows Brian." Jack's eyes shift to my face. "Why?"

I can feel the pulse in my wrist thumping up against my skin. The words are locked in my head. *Just ask him, Linda. Ask if he knows how to contact him.*

I shrug. In the last few days, I've told Jack practically my entire life history. I don't know why I can't do this.

"You're not going to tell me you've been involved with him, are you?" Jack teases.

Everything inside me freezes suddenly. I shake my head.

"No. My name is Linda Cray," I blurt out.

Jack's gaze sharpens. I don't know what he sees on my face, but he pulls to the side of the road, the tires squealing as the car abruptly stops. He is studying me, those penetrating blues eyes probing, relentless, and I look away.

Damn, why didn't I wait? We're less than a handful of miles

from home. And instinct is telling me I don't want this scene somewhere not private.

"Of fuck. Is that why you're with me? Is that what this is about?" he asks, his voice gritty and raw.

I turn to lock eyes with his. I can't speak. The emotions are flashing too quickly on his face for me to read any of them clearly.

His fingers tighten around the steering wheel. "Jesus Christ, you're his daughter, aren't you?"

I feel like I'm about to hyperventilate. I fumble for the door handle. "I need to get out. I need air."

He grabs my arm. "You're not going anywhere until you explain every part of this to me."

My cheeks burn. "Explain what?"

His eyes can dissect like a hawk hunting for prey. I grow even colder inside.

"On the beach," he says. I don't at all like what's in his tone. "Was that an accident or some kind of setup to get close to me? How long have you been playing me?"

"Playing you?" I frown and shuck in a few quick breaths of air. "I wasn't playing you! Playing you for what?"

"You are a beautiful woman. You can have any man you want," he says in a whisper, but his expression is the opposite— enraged. "You're only here with me because you want something from me. Isn't that how girls like you work?"

"Girls like me?" I choke out.

His gaze sharpens. "Groupie. All the musicians you've been with. It's almost your profession. Do you really attend USC, or is that just something to spice up your narrative?"

He says it like a man solving a riddle: detached, cold.

I can tell by how he's watching me that there is no point in lying. He can read me too well, there is just the right amount of truth in his observations, that anything less than total honesty he will never believe.

"How long have you been playing me?" he demands, his fingers clenching tighter on the steering wheel.

I stare down at my hands, folded in my lap. "It didn't start that way. Not in the beginning. I just found you on the beach. I didn't even know for sure who you were until later…"

"How much later?"

I snap up my face to look at him. "Inside the house. When I saw Lily."

He sinks back into his seat, his limbs in a more open posture, his fingers slowly relaxing their grip of the steering wheel.

"So you decided to stick around. Play attentive, accommodating girlfriend. You want me to tell you where your father is! You've been trading your body to find your father. Trading favors for help, so to speak?"

That's it. Without thought, I slap him. My hand instantly starts to burn, and I swivel in my seat, fighting to open the door.

I stumble out of the car, barely managing to stay on my feet. I run through the tall weeds until my legs can no longer carry me and I sink onto the dirt, breathing heavily and trying to reign in my spinning thoughts and emotions.

Furiously, I brush at my tears. There is nothing Jack said that should have offended me. It's all true. But hearing him say the unvarnished truth hurt me so badly because—*oh god*—I love him. I've let myself be lured out of my safe zone far enough to fall in love with him.

Goddammit, I let myself fall in love with Jackson Parker! How stupid can I be? This is not how this was supposed to go.

A week-long affair and then neatly over. I'm supposed to have some fun. He's supposed to be amused by me. I'm supposed to get from him the location of my father and he's supposed to watch me leave.

An encounter: beginning, middle and end, with no hurt hearts on either side. That's how these flings go. They are not supposed to end with *me* loving *him*.

As I hug my legs with my arms and try to hold my shaking limbs steady, I hear faint footsteps closing in on me. *Fuck, he's following me.* It would have been better for us both if he just drove off and dumped me here.

Now, I have to face him with the truth of my deception and the truth of my heart.

From close behind me, I hear his husky, gentle voice say, "Why don't you start at the beginning and tell me truth about everything?"

I bury my face in my hands. The words bubble up and I can't stop them.

"I know you don't have any reason to believe me, but I didn't play you. Well, not after the first day because everything changed. At least for me it changed. I'm in love with you, so if you're going to tell me off, can you please do it quickly and go away?"

I hear a heavy sigh and I can feel his stare. He's moved to stand before me, and I haven't yet looked at him.

"If you're ready to talk, I'm ready to listen," he offers quietly.

That's it? That's all he has to say to me after all the horrible things I've done?

"I don't know if I want to tell you anything."

I sound just a touch pouty and I hate that. It makes me sound young and weak and I don't want him to think that I'm either.

He sinks down beside me on the dirt and takes me into his arms. At the first touch I melt against his chest and the tears return.

He waits until the tears stop, then gives me a slight squeeze. "It's going to be OK. Nothing is ever as terrible as we think it is."

Cautiously, I look up at him. "If you believe that, you're lucky. Everything always proves to be *more* terrible than I think it is."

Jack laughs tenderly. "In all moments a wisecrack. It's all going to be OK. You've got to start having faith in something at some point in your life. Why not now?"

His gentleness, his affection for me, is reflected in his eyes. This is the biggest part of us that I don't grasp. It's illogical. It all makes it impossible for me to let down my guard enough to believe he's giving me what I can see he is offering me.

His eyes say he cares for me. My fragile heart says *Why me?* Why would the man who can have anyone, let me in and care for me?

I sniffle and lay my cheek back against his shirt. "I'm sorry."

"Don't be. I'm not. I may not like how we started, but I sure like where we are."

I don't trust myself enough to speak. I nervously peek up at him. He smiles at me.

"Why don't we go home and figure this out together," he murmurs.

I curl back into his chest, hiding my face. "I'd rather go

home to bed," I tease softly.

I peek up at him again.

He raises his eyebrows slightly, looks a touched amused, and then shakes his head.

"You haven't figured out my code yet." His voice is suggestive. "I didn't say we'd start with figuring this out together."

I give a soggy laugh and he drops a kiss on the top of my head. He stands and holds out a hand to me.

"Come." Taking his hand, he helps guide me onto my feet.

This contact, flesh to flesh, is everything I've ever dreamed of with a man. Normal and tender and intimate and kind.

His arm slips protectively around my waist as we slug through the high weeds back to the car. I can't reconcile this wonderful man being here with me, but maybe it's time to stop fighting it.

He opens my door. He kisses my cheek. "I want to go home, make love to you, and then finally meet Linda Cray."

His husky voice brushes my senses like a caress. The look in his eyes melts my heart. Suddenly, I'm completely lost in my emotions for him.

I place a light kiss on his hand curled over the top of the car door.

I look up. "How do you do? I'm Linda Cray."

"I'm Jackson Parker," he says simply, gazing at me with his famous blue eyes shimmering, "and I am in love with you."

CHAPTER TEN

Day 12...

I sit on the chaise lounge I dragged to the edge of the lawn above the cliffs and watch Jack dart in and out of the water on a surfboard.

I've missed an entire week of classes. Jeanette is pissed off at me and warning that the USC wants to talk me about my scholarship. And I am not troubled in the least about the mess I'm making of my life.

Right now, I am totally willing to let every part of my world crash and burn to indulge this delicious fantasy. Every minute with Jack is filled with him.

I went to sleep last night a rational girl with thoughts in my head of telling Jack I have to go home in the morning.

He roused me from sleep shortly before dawn, whispering something about glassy and the waves being good. He made love to my drowsy, warm body, and left me.

I went back to sleep afterwards, a woman in love, curled

around his pillow, desperate to stay.

We are everything a couple should be and everything I've never experienced before with a man. I am head over heels in love with him and there are moments now that I actually believe he is in love with me.

Jack would call that progress, kiss me on the lips, and then smile.

For me, it's a little sad and it makes me angry. Even in this very unexpectedly wonderful thing I've stumbled into, I can't seem to let myself be completely happy.

I wish I knew if finding my father would at last end all the unwanted conflict in me. If I were done with Bray Cray, once and for all, would I be able to love Jack as effortlessly as he loves me?

I'm starting to get frantic and impatient for that answer. I wish I knew if Jack were looking for my father. Jack seems not the least bit inclined to discuss any of this and I don't push from my end. We are happy.

He loves me. Jackson Parker is in love with me.

God, I love hearing it in my head, even though it still sounds strange to me.

Jack is sitting, waiting for a wave, and I smile at him even though he can't see me. Men and their amusements. I usually find them confounding and irritating, but in every breath Jack is wonderful. Part man, part boy, but always deliciously him. And he definitely looks hot in that wetsuit.

I grab my coffee cup and wrap my fingers around it to keep them warm. He jogs out of the surf, drops his board in the sand, and sprints up those treacherous steps to me.

As he crosses the lawn, I smile. "Aren't you afraid someone will steal your board leaving it down there?"

Jack laughs and grabs the towel draped over the back of the chair. "Not in the least. If they take it, they need it and that's OK with me."

I roll my eyes at his '60s outlook on everything. It's easy to have a positive outlook on everything if you've always had money. I wonder if he knows how philosophically illogical he is.

I bite my lip to prevent the taunt. My taunts have become a part of our familiar teasing. He's in a good mood. I don't want to spar with him today. I just want to be nice and love him.

He sinks down on the chaise beside me, vigorously drying his hair with a towel.

I pull away from him, fighting the droplets of ocean water hitting me. "You're wet and cold. Get away from me."

"I'm hot and ready beneath the neoprene. Can I stay?" he teases, dropping a kiss on my nose.

I blush. "Only if you take it off."

"Aha. A woman who thinks like me."

He stands up, unzips it halfway, and starts pulling the sleeve from one arm.

"You're not taking it off out here!"

Those blue eyes glow wickedly. "I would if you wanted me to, baby."

He tries to kiss me, but I laugh and push him away. He continues undressing and my eyes round.

He smiles, shaking his head. "I'm just getting a little air. You work up a sweat out there. Besides, I already worked up a sweat with you this morning and I have other plans for us today."

He eases it down until the top half of the suit hangs from his hips. The tanned muscles of his chest glisten with a light mist of perspiration. I lean in to put a kiss beside his navel, my senses savoring the smell and taste of him.

I rub my cheek against his flesh. He *is* warm beneath the suit. My eyes stray lower, wondering if he is ready as well, and my face colors.

He settles down beside me and folds me into his arms. "How long will it take you to shower, dress and pack? I want to get on the road early. It's a six hour drive to San Francisco."

My eyes widen in surprise. "San Francisco? Why are we going there today?"

His arms tighten in their hold as he drops a kiss on my head. "I found your father. He's been living in San Francisco for twenty years. Today we are going to visit Brian Cray."

We are both strangely quiet during the long car ride up the 101 toward San Francisco. The day is gorgeous and the ride a beautiful blend of coastline, farmland, tiny cities and nothing. The somberness in the car seems out of place.

It's just before 6 p.m. in the evening before I catch my first glimpse of the city and the bay. I've never been to San Francisco before and I wish I was coming knowing for certain it would be a good thing.

For some reason, when Jack finally reached my father and mentioned he'd be stopping by this weekend, he didn't mention it was with me. Jack made sure I knew this, though I'm not exactly sure why.

I study the hilly streets with buildings that look so different from LA, and the people who look even more different, as we go deeper into the city.

I don't have a clue where I am or the journey that got me here. I'd probably be freaking out right now if Jack wasn't sitting beside me.

I look over at him and smile.

Jack's fingers close around my fingers and he touches them to his lips.

"Do you want to check into the hotel first or go directly to the studio and see your dad?" he asks.

I make a snap decision. I want to get this over with. Any more thinking and I might lose my courage.

"My dad first."

Jack studies my face. "Are you sure? We've been driving for hours. It wouldn't hurt to rest and have something to eat."

I tense. He's concerned for some reason. What is he trying to prepare me for?

"No. I want to do this. I've waited a long time to meet my dad. I don't want to put this off."

Jack nods and continues to drive.

Thirty minutes later, we're parking in front of a shabby, old store type of building.

Jack springs from the car and runs around it to open my door.

"This doesn't look very glamorous for a recording studio," I freely tease. "I thought my dad was very high demand."

Jack laughs. "He is." He looks up at the city with a slight smile. "But this is San Francisco. Space anywhere you can get it."

The entry of the shop is dark. There is no reception desk and it looks almost abandoned. We walk down a narrow hallway toward the back of the building and stop at a heavy soundproof door.

When I enter the control room, it is silent and empty, but I can see through the glass a man is stretched out on a sofa, smoking.

I conclude they must be on break or something. Probably a dinner break.

I stare through the glass. So that's him. He looks older than I expected him to, but then I remember Doris is older now, as well. He has dark curls and dark eyes, and bears a slight resemblance to me. The nose and the eyes yes. But the rest of me, I think must be Doris, because I don't see myself in him in any other way.

What a strange feeling it is, to see him and be near him. I expected to feel something different. Some instant connection to confirm that we are related. I feel only a vague sense of anger and a greater sense of fear.

"Come on," Jacks says quietly.

He takes my hand and pushes through the control room door. Brian Cray startles, opens his eyes, fixes on Jack, and springs to his feet.

"Jack," my father says, rushing across the studio, quickly extending a hand. "You are a surprise I wasn't expecting when you called this morning. How long are you two in the city?"

Jack's arm tightens around my shoulder. "Just the weekend. This beautiful young woman wanted to meet you."

Brian looks at me in a curious and nothing sort of way. He laughs. "I can't imagine why. You're the legend here. I'm just a drummer for hire."

He laughs and doesn't seem to notice that neither Jack nor I laugh with him.

"We've already met once," I hear myself whisper in a thin

93

voice that sounds weirdly far away.

Brian's dark brows shoot up. "Really? I think you're mistaken. I can't imagine that I would forget your face."

"I was seven. We bumped into each other at a store. I was with my mother. Doris."

He stares at me. I see the moment he figures it out and the moment he pretends he doesn't by smiling.

"Really? I'm sorry. I don't recall. That would have been a long time ago."

I am suddenly drowning in more truthful fact about my dad than Doris has ever shared with me.

"No. Why should you? I'm only your daughter for Christ's sake."

He frowns and then smiles in a falsely pleased kind of way. "Linda. Well look at you. You can't fault me for not recognizing you. It's been a long time and you've certainly grown up into a lovely young woman." He looks at Jack. "Hasn't she? Well, if this isn't a mind blower. How'd the two of you hook up? Is your mom still living in Venice Beach? I always did like Doris. She's well, I hope."

I stare at him with my mouth slightly dropping.

Insincere, dismissive pleasantries dripping and oozing from an asshole. That's what my dad is. This is the man who abandoned me, and whom Doris has glorified by passing the years pining over him.

Brian Cray is nothing like my mother described. He's an *asshole*.

Oh shit. Oh shit. Oh Shit.

My heart is pounding in my chest like an iron mallet, and I'm starting to hyperventilate.

Brian Cray couldn't care less that I am here or that I am his daughter. I don't know what I expected at this moment, but it was never that. I never expected my father to dismiss me.

I run from the building without a word, and I don't stop until I'm on the street. Walking in circles, shaking my hands, I try to stop the chaotic, free-falling emotion inside me.

I thought I would feel better if I could just find my dad and tell him off. But I don't. I feel worse. Different. Like suddenly every piece of me is no longer connected, comfortable or steady.

I've worked three years for this moment and now that it's here I wish I had never bothered.

I brush furiously at my tears and try to steady my shaking body. Warm hands slip over my shoulders and I am turned into Jack's chest and he is holding me.

My fingers curl around his shirt and my body won't stop shaking. If Jack wasn't holding me, I'd be on the ground now.

I start to cry harder. "I want to go home. I want to leave here now."

He kisses me gently all over my face as he brushes away my tears. "We will, baby. We'll go home. Just calm down and let me take you there."

We reach Santa Barbara shortly after two a.m. Jack carries me into the house, lays me on the bed, and surrounds me with his warmth and limbs.

"It will be all right, Linda," he whispers, his lips buried into my hair. "Just rest, baby. Everything will seem better in the morning and we'll figure out everything then."

I turn into him, burying my face against his chest. I don't even have tears anymore. I just need to be as close to Jack as possible and have him hold me.

CHAPTER ELEVEN

Shortly before dawn, I slip out of Jack's arms and into the bathroom, carefully closing the door not to wake him. I am finally calm enough to call my mother.

I sink on the tile floor and reach for that silly wall mounted phone near the toilet.

It's probably too early to call Doris. But if I wait, she might leave for the restaurant and I'll miss her until the end of the day. The need to talk to my mother is too urgent to wait.

I reach for the receiver and punch in my mom's number.

Two rings. Answered. Good, she's already awake.

"Hello?"

"Hi, Mom."

"Linda—" I scrunch up my face. When she draws my name out loudly and long it means something has worried her about me. "—where are you? I called Jeannette and she said she didn't know. In Santa Barbara was all she said. The school called me. They want to talk to you about your scholarship. What kind of trouble are you in this time?"

I fight back the urge to cry. "No trouble, Mom. I'm OK. I'll be home today. I'll fix things with school. You don't have to worry. I just needed to take care of something."

A long exhale of breath.

"OK, huh?" A pause. She smacks her lips the way she does when she's not buying anything I say. "Aha. You're OK, you've been MIA for nearly two weeks, and your education is just about in the crapper. But I'm supposed to believe that something isn't wrong. Why do I suspect there's a guy involved in this?"

"Because you know me," I tease hopefully.

I scrunch up my face. Doris is upset. I shouldn't be making wisecracks.

"Linda, Linda, Linda. What am I going to do with you?"

I start to cry. "Just love me, Mom."

A longer silence.

"Linda, what's wrong?" Doris says now her voice more soothing. "Why is my girl crying? You never cry."

I sniff. "It's nothing, Mom. Hey, I'm going to stop in Reseda on my way back to school. Do you think you could get off early and be there?"

"Why, Linda? What's wrong?"

I rub my nose against my dripping nose. "Nothing, Mom. I just need to see you. Have I ever told you you're a pretty great mom?"

Doris laughs, half in amusement, half in frustration.

"Nope. Can't say that you have. I'll see you this afternoon."

"Around three?"

"I'll try. I've got to run. I'm going to be late for work. I'm opening the restaurant today."

"OK, Mom. Bye."

I set down the receiver and return it to the wall. I lean my head back to stare at the skylight over me.

I climb slowly to my feet and pause at the sink to splash water in my face. I stare at myself in the mirror.

It's time to go home. There are things I need to take care of with my mother. Jack's daughter is returning tomorrow. He has things to take care of with her as well.

I pat my face dry with a towel and grab a tissue from the box to blow my nose. I toss it into the pretty crystal shell waste can.

I re-enter the bedroom and Jack is awake. He looks at me, smiles touching both his lips and eyes.

Before he can speak, I say, "How long do you think it will take to get a car and driver here? I need to go back to Reseda."

I sink to the floor on my knees and start to grab my clothes from the chair to shove them into my shopping bag.

"Linda, what are you doing?"

I can't look at him. "It's time for me to leave. Your daughter comes home tomorrow. I have to get back to school. We had fun, but now it's time I move on."

I listen to his movements behind me. He doesn't come to me. He's sitting on the bed.

"No, baby. There is no reason for you to leave. What are you thinking? How could you want to go?"

I don't want to go! As perfect as we are together it is not our time. Right man. Wrong time. Wrong for me. Wrong for him, only he can't see it, and that's one of the reasons I am so desperately in love with him.

"I can't just run off. I've got my mother. My education. I graduate in spring."

I stand up and push the hair from my face.

I look at him.

"Please call me a car, Jack. Don't make this harder than it is for me."

The perfect lines of his face stiffen. "I'll call, Linda. But we are going to talk this out. We are not over and I don't want you to leave."

I nod. I don't want this to be the end of us forever. It may be the wrong time, but I am far from ready to let him go.

I grab an outfit to wear today.

"Would you mind if I took a long bath in your fancy tub?"

I don't wait for him to answer. I dart back into the bathroom and lock the door between us.

There is a knock on the door.

"The car is here, Linda, but I expect you to come out and talk to me before you try to leave."

I stare at my reflection in the full wall mirror. I've been dressed for over an hour. I can't hide in here forever.

Jack is sitting on the foot of the bed facing me when I exit the bathroom.

"You've been very kind," I whisper. "I don't know how I'll ever be able to thank you for everything you've done for me."

His magnificent blue eyes lock on me.

"Stay."

I struggle to hold back the tears.

"I can't stay. I need to go back to LA, have a heart-to-heart with my mother, and then figure out how to save my scholarship."

"You don't have to do this alone. I can help you."

"I don't need help. Not now. I've done what I set out to do, Jack. I've found my father and I'm not letting Brian Cray take one more thing from me."

"Maybe this time he didn't take from you. Maybe he gave. You found me."

Oh god, I have to get out of here, out of here quickly or I will walk out on my scholarship to USC just to stay here with this man.

As wonderful as Jack is, it will end the same as all my relationships do; it will end badly with him moving on to the next girl. That's what always happens.

Be smart, Linda. For once, be the girl who walks away.

My legs feel weak and shaky as I step closer to the door and away from him. "I had a wonderful time with you, but I'm going home. We're over."

Jack starts to quietly laugh and he closes the space between us. He takes my face in the cradle of his palms. "Oh no, Linda. We're not over. I'm a guy who knows when he's met forever."

I stare up at him, my heart in my throat, and I don't know how to answer that.

Jack surrounds me with his body, his arms braced on the door, his scent sending my senses into a frenzy as slowly he starts the dangerous decent of his mouth to mine. "One last kiss, Linda. *Then* tell me you're going to walk away."

Our passion ignites at the first touch of our lips and every part of me is instantly lost in him. My legs and arms lose their strength and I can feel myself in a fast free-fall, losing my power to leave him.

I twist out of his arms and step back quickly. I feel a stinging burn on my cheeks and realize my tears are flowing from my eyes in fierce currents.

"I can't stay, Jack. If I do it means I've learned nothing from watching my mother. And I don't think I can live with that."

He brushes away my tears with both his lips and his thumbs. Then, he gives back the space between us.

"Leaving won't make a difference about anything. It won't make you a smarter woman and it won't make us over. It'll only make you gone. We are far from over, Linda, and we both know it."

I stare at the pretty bright foil Back Street shopping bags and fumble to open the bedroom door. I feel the truth of his words in my core. By the time I reach the front porch, I'm breathing like I've just run a marathon and my arms and legs have lost all sensation.

The driver sprints around the black Town car and opens the door for me. Frantically, I look over my shoulder toward the heavy wooden front door I left open. I'm relieved that Jack didn't follow. I don't know if I'd have the will to climb into the car if he did.

I duck as I settle into the plush leather backseat. I look at the front door one last time. How easy it would be to step back into the house and run down the hall to Jack.

The slam of the car door makes me jump, and a few moments later my numb senses grow aware we are moving. I stare out the tinted passenger window, my teary eyes blurring and distorting the gorgeous, peaceful view.

Maybe Jack is right: I don't know how to let a man be good to me.

~~~The End~~~

Thank you for reading. For more books in An Affair Without End Series check my website http://www.susanwardbooks.com/ for release dates. Or you can can follow me on twitter @susaninlaguna or like me on Facebook: https://www.facebook.com/susanwardbooks?ref=hl

EXCERPTS

If you enjoyed One Last Kiss, you may enjoy The Girl on the Half Shell available now on Amazon, as the Parker Family Saga continues. Please enjoy the following excerpt:

The room is so quiet it is deafening.

I find Alan on his bed, casually reclined against a stack of pillows, dressed only in flannel pajama bottoms, and reading—of all things—the *Wall Street Journal*. There is a fire lit, the silver candlesticks flicker with flame, the bedcovers invitingly turned down as if in preparation for some sort of romantic scene. But he is focused on the *Journal*.

He doesn't look at me and I feel stupid hovering by his door, so I start to wander around the bedroom, trying to still my frantic pulse. It's a good thing that it's an interesting room, otherwise my deliberate study would seem silly.

Even Alan's bedroom is something I find weird and demands a certain amount of mental analysis. It looks something from a nineteenth century English manor, elegant to the point of being almost a touch prissy. There's an antique mahogany king-sized bed facing the fireplace; floral wingback chairs with pillows positioned before the hearth; and high-tech conveniences camouflaged in antique furniture. There's a Monet on the wall; tall, polished sterling silver candlesticks; crystal; and fine, leather-bound, first edition books of classic literature. I sink down before a small, mahogany table where I find a stack of newspaper: *Barons*; the *New York Times*; the *Washington Post*; and the *Daily Telegraph*.

The warmth of the fire surrounds me like a caress, but I am quaking like a leaf. I wasn't sure what Alan expected after he walked out of the kitchen. It would have been logical to assume that I would leave. But he knew I'd follow him. I don't know why he's ignoring me now. I look at the lit candlesticks—he wanted me to follow him.

I bite my lower lip and stare at my knotted fingers. I stayed alone in the kitchen for what seemed like ages, and now that I've done exactly what he expected me to do, *nothing*.

I struggle for something to say to break the silence. "You do have seven bedrooms. I counted them twice. But there are seven only if I include yours."

He folds the *Journal*, tosses it on the table and fixes those penetrating, mesmerizing eyes on me. "Is this the room you want?" he asks, his voice gentle. "I meant it when I said you could have any room. It doesn't have to be my room for you to stay."

Does he not want me in his room? A ragged breath forces its way from deep in my lungs. "Do you want me to go?" I murmur.

"Of course not. I want you here." His voice is husky and his eyes are wandering in a leisurely hold that is tender and oddly comforting.

Thank you for reading. You might enjoy a sneak peek into Chrissie and Alan's future, with Rewind A Perfect Forever Novella. Available now on Amazon:

He doesn't laugh. Instead, his gaze sharpens on my face. "I am being nice, Kaley. I came to you. I got tired of waiting."

What? Did I just hear what I think I heard?

Before I can respond, he says, "How's your afternoon looking? Do you have time to take off and come see something with me?"

My afternoon? There is something. I'm sure of that, but I suddenly can't remember a single thing.

"What do you have in mind?"

"I want to show you where I've been living. What's I've been doing? I think you'll find it interesting."

Interesting? Why would I find it interesting?

"So, do you think you can cut out for a few hours?" he asks, watching me expectantly.

I focus my gaze on the table, wondering if I should go, wondering why I debate this, and what the heck I have on calendar that I can't remember. God this is weird, familiar and distant at once, and I haven't a clue what I should do here.

I stare at his hand, so close to mine, on the table. Whoever thought it would be so uncomfortable *not* to touch a guy? It doesn't feel natural this space we hold between us, spiced with the kind of talk people have who know each other intimately. What would he do if I touched him...?

His fingers cover mine and he gives me a friendly squeeze. The feel of him runs through my body with remember sweetness.

Suddenly, nothing in my life is as important as spending the afternoon with Bobby and for the first time, in a very long time, I don't feel like a disjointed collection of uncomfortably fitting parts. I feel at ease inside me being with Bobby.

I stop trying to access my mental calendar. I smile up at Bobby. "I've got as much time as you need."

Bobby chuckles and his hand slips back from me. He rises and tosses some bills on the table. "Just a few hours, Kaley. I'll have you back before the end of the day."

I rise from my chair and think *not if I figure out fast how not to blow this.*

Thank you for reading. Continue the story of Chrissie and Alan in the second book of the Half Shell Series: Girl of Tokens and Tears coming Fall 2014. Please enjoy the following sneak peek as Neil Stanton re-enters the story:

"Here, you look like you could use this," says a quiet male voice above me.

I look up only far enough to see the carry size pack of tissue held out in long, tan fingers. I take one and anxiously dab at my tears. On the concrete walkway below there is a pair of some kind of work shoe and dark blue pant legs that look like they belong to a jump suit or something. Oh God, the janitor I barreled into. How humiliating is this? To be the girl alone on a concrete slab, crying and being consoled by the janitor.

I don't look up, praying he'll go away.

"Can I sit on your bench?" he asks politely.

I nod. "It's not my bench and it's a free country."

He gives me a small laugh for that. I avoid looking straight at him, inhale another sniffle, and touch my nose with the tissue.

"Thank you. You've been very nice," I whisper.

He settles near me copying my posture, feet on bench, legs bent and facing me.

"You know, Lambert will only bully you if you let him," he advises kindly. "And he only bullies the students he thinks have potential they are not putting to good use."

"Thanks. I'll try to remember that. He doesn't hate me. I have potential."

He laughs and from a pack on the ground he takes a brown lunch bag and sets it beside him.

"Rough year?" He is carefully unwrapping some kind of minimart precooked burrito thing.

Jeez, is he going to eat that cold?

"Do you want a bite? It isn't a terrible as it looks."

I start to laugh when I really don't want to. "Thanks, but no thanks!"

"Come on. What's not to love? Week old beans. Week old rice and I'm not even sure what the sauce is. Be bold. Be brave. Eat a minimart burrito from yesterday."

Ok, that was funny. I look at him then locking on green eyes and I see a really sweet teasing glint in them. His eyes are large, brightly colored and filled with a smile. Shoulder length blond streaked brown hair peeks out from beneath an army green bandana and the face of the janitor is tanned, really good looking...and really familiar.

Why does it feel like I know him?

"Are you homesick? Is that why you mope around campus all day?"

I lift my chin. "I don't mope and how would you know what I do all day?"

He takes the keys hanging from his belt and shakes them. "There's not much to do when you push a broom in the music department except listen and watch everything." He takes a bite of his burrito. "You have Lambert's class from 10 until 11. You sit on this bench until noon. You have a practice room from 1 until 2. You sit on this bench until 3. You have your lab with Jared the TA—who is hot for you, would really like to date you, and is afraid to ask—that's at 3:30. And then sometimes you do another hour in a practice room, but most times you disappear from campus. You are back at 7 for symphony. That's your Tuesday/Thursday schedule."

My eyes round and I tense. Jeez, maybe he's not just the janitor. Maybe he's a stalker or something!

"How do you know all that?" I ask fearfully.

"I push a broom, remember?" he replies casually.

I start to gather my things.

"Hey," he says putting his hand on my arm. "You don't have to run for security, Chrissie. I would never hurt a hometown girl. The rest of the girls I stalk are in trouble, but you're pretty much safe. We've got that whole SB thing going on. Like comrades bonded in warfare."

His boyish eyes start to twinkle above an endearing smile. I stare at him. Chrissie: he knows my name. SB thing? He's from Santa Barbara too. I study him more closely and I just can't place the face. I know I know the face, but I'm not connecting the dots, and I'm not tapping into that instinct thing telling me if I use to like him or I should run.

He frowns. "Now I'm hurt."

Crap, he can see I'm not remembering him.

He tosses his unfinished burrito into the bag. "Do you forget every really, really cool guy who does you a really, really big favor?"

I feel my heart drop to my knees. *Really, really cool guy*....Oh crap! Neil Stanton. Yep, I definitely remember him. The jerk from that night Rene and I went clubbing at Peppers before spring break. The guy who thought he needed to give me life advice after making a fool out of me. In my memory I can still hear him saying *Didn't Daddy teach you anything about how the world works.*

Or enjoy the first novel in the Perfect Forever Novels: The Signature. Available Now. Please enjoy the following excerpt from The Signature:

She became aware all at once how utterly delightful it felt to be here with him, alone on the quay, with the erotic nearness of his body.

She closed her eyes. "Listen to the quiet. There are times when I lie here and it feels like there is no one else in the world."

"No one else in the world? Would that be a good thing?" he asked thoughtfully.

"No. But the illusion is grand, don't you think?" she whispered.

Krystal turned her head to the side, lifting her lids to find Devon's gaze sparkling as he studied her. He shook his head lazily. "No. The illusion wouldn't be grand at all. It would mean I wasn't here with you."

It all changed at once, yet again, and so quickly that Krystal couldn't stop it. The ticklish feeling stirred in her limbs. Devon's words, as well as the closeness of their bodies, should have sent her into active retreat, and instead she felt herself wanting to curl into him. *What would it feel like if kissed me? Would I still feel this delicious inside? Or would that old panic and fear return?*

Laughing softly, Devon said, "I'm not used to relaxing. Can you tell?"

"I wasn't used to it before Coos Bay, either. There is a different pace of life here. At first I thought there was no sound. That's how quiet it seemed to me. Then I realized that there is music, beautiful music in this quiet."

After a long pause, he murmured, "You'll have to bring me here every Saturday until I learn to hear music in the quiet."

Krystal smiled. "Once you hear the music it's perfect."

"It's perfect now to me." His voice was a husky, sensual whisper.

He was on his side facing her. *When had that happened?* An inadvertent thrill ran through her flesh, and she could see it in his eyes—the supplication, the want, and an unexplainable reluctance to indulge either.

Devon was no longer smiling, his eyes had become brighter

and more diffuse. His fingertips started to trace her face with such exquisite lightness that her insides shook. For the first time, in a very long time, she felt completely a woman and wanting.

Was it possible? Had she finally healed internally as her flesh had done so long ago? Was she finally past the legacy of Nick? Was what she was now feeling real? Should she seek the answer with Devon? Or was it better to leave it unexplored?

"You are a very beautiful woman," he whispered.

She watched with sleepy movements as his mouth lowered to her. It came first as a touch on her cheek, feather soft between the play of his fingers. Her breath caught, followed by a pleasant quickening of her pulse. She was unprepared for the sweetness of his lips and the rushing sensations that ran her body. His thumb traced the lines of her mouth, as his kiss moved sweetly, gently there.

His breath became rapid in a way that matched her own, and his mouth grew fuller and more searching. The fingertips curving her chin were like a gentle embrace, but their mouths were eager and demanding. Flashes of desire rocketed through her powerfully. Urgency sang through her flesh, a forgotten melody, now in vibrant notes. She found herself wanting to twist into him. Reality begged her to twist back.

ABOUT THE AUTHOR

Susan Ward is a native of Santa Barbara, California, where she currently lives in a house on the side of a mountain, overlooking the Pacific Ocean. She doesn't believe she makes sense anywhere except near the sea. She attended the University of California Santa Barbara and earned a degree in Business Administration from California State University Sacramento. She works as a Government Relations Consultant, focusing on issues of air quality and global warming. The mother of grown daughters, she lives a quiet life with her husband and her dog Emma. She can be found most often walking at Hendry's Beach, where she writes most of her storylines in her head while watching Emma play in the surf.

Spare a tree. Be good to the earth. Donate or share my books with a friend.